MASQUE OF BLOOD

Murder on the South Downs

JOHN PICK

Designed and Illustrated by

JANE MONTAGUE

Grosvenor House
Publishing Limited

The right of John Pick to be identified as the author of this
work has been asserted in accordance with Section 78
of the Copyright, Designs and Patents Act 1988

The book cover is copyright to Jane Montague, RIBA

This book is published by
Grosvenor House Publishing Ltd
Link House
140 The Broadway, Tolworth, Surrey, KT6 7HT.
www.grosvenorhousepublishing.co.uk

This book is a work of fiction. Any resemblance to
people or events, past or present, is purely coincidental.

A CIP record for this book
is available from the British Library

ISBN 978-1-78623-451-3

ACKNOWLEDGEMENTS

I would like, as always, to thank the brilliant Jane Montague for her many contributions to this little fantasy, and the sharp-eyed John Pleydell, for reading a draft and almost certainly saving me from having to defend myself in a court of law.

Speaking of which, I should like to say that although the settings are real enough, none of the characters is a representation of any person, living or half-dead. Some of the titles are also invented. There is, for example, no such position as Assistant Police and Law Commissioner for the South East Region.

Nor do the horrible crimes depicted herein refer, directly or metaphorically, to anything which has ever happened on the Sunshine Coast. So far.

JP

ONE

Someone or something was licking his right ear.

With an effort, he prised one eye open. From the blankets arranged over Ben's wheelchaired lap, Snuff was looking up at him, tongue lolling reproachfully. The dog had no notion why they were up here on the Downs on a cold autumn night, yet he sensed that they should not both be asleep. But now, seeing that one of his master's rheumy eyes was on him, the ageing hound settled back and resumed his slumbers, satisfied that he had played his part in the night's activities.

In the darkness Detective Inspector Ben Jackson-Grant (Retired) raised the other eyelid, rubbed both eye sockets with a gloved hand and perfunctorily wiped his ear. He fumbled beneath the wheelchair's blankets for his binoculars – his cover story was that he was a twitcher logging the night lives of the South Downs birds – and then peered down the slope to the lay-by thirty feet below.

It was still empty.

The sky was dark and heavy, the moon obscured by scudding clouds. A faint breeze coming off the Channel stirred the thin twigs of his makeshift hide. From far off, towards Newhaven, came the deep melancholy note of a ship's foghorn, like some Jurassic sea monster breaking wind.

Ben glanced at the watch his colleagues had pressed on him at his retirement, with its busy panel of pointless information. It was, he noticed, 17.30 hrs in Washington, and half past ten here on the South Downs. At least two hours before Julia would release him from his shadowy hiding place.

A sudden mechanical whirring as a partridge took wing away over the farmland.

On his lap the sleeping dog snored and after a few seconds growled idiotically at the sound it had made. Fumbling in the darkness Ben located his flask and gradually eased it out, conscious of the clumsiness of his gloved hands. He eased open the cap and dribbled steaming coffee into the plastic cup.

Only then did he see, from the corner of his eye, the powerful white headlights approaching, unhurriedly, from the Eastbourne direction. He balanced his coffee in the holder on the wheelchair arm, raised his binoculars and looked along the road, hearing the purr of its engine grow. The lights dipped and grew larger as the vehicle came into view, glided past the Countryside Centre and the pub, slowing as it approached the lay-by.

Just as Julia had said might happen.

He watched as the vehicle eased itself smoothly into the recess below, stopped, shut off its lights and then fell silent.

It was a police car, all right. In the brief reflection of its lights on the low stone wall, Ben had been able to register the familiar markings. So far so good. From his long experience he knew that a lookout must take nothing for granted. Nevertheless, things looked promising. As he had been told would happen, and at about the right time, a police car had indeed pulled up in the expected place.

He sipped his coffee and waited. All that could be heard was some animal scuffing the topsoil near to the cliff edge. There was no sound or movement from the car.

It could, of course just be coincidence - a bored night patrol pulling off the road for a quiet fag and a sarnie. There would be nothing unusual in that.

Until, without warning, a figure slithered out of the rear offside door, closed it quietly, looked both ways along the road and then, apparently satisfied with what it saw, struck a match and lit a cigarette.

So what? These days all police cars carried smoke detectors, so if you wanted a quick drag you had to get out. But in the brief flare of the match Ben had seen something that was significant. The figure that emerged from the car appeared to be wearing a white shirt and tie.

Not uniformed then. Nor was he one of the plain-clothes lot either. They wouldn't turn out at this time of night, unless it was a major job, and the lack of action in the lay-by did not suggest they were on their way to a big one. Or could the figure be somebody being taken in for questioning, let out here for a quiet smoke?

No, even less likely.

For a moment Ben even allowed himself to believe the figure was familiar to him, someone he knew. But it was too dark, too shadowy, too ill-defined for that to be more than a passing fancy. He put the thought from his mind.

He looked again at his watch. Twenty to eleven. He double-checked the time on his smartphone, shielding its dim light behind his scarf. Below him, the figure was leaning on the roof of the car, taking long puffs on the glowing cigarette.

Then the sound of a car, also coming out from Eastbourne, thumping out some raucous din from its radio. Students, he thought disapprovingly. The figure froze but as the vehicle thudded past he thought he saw, in its headlights, twin glints from the smoker's eyes. The figure was wearing spectacles.

He heard sounds, but it was only the voices of the ladies of the Beachy Head Patrol, as they walked along the cliff top, intent on saving the immortal souls of the would-be suicides. They sounded bored. Too cold tonight to top yourself, Ben thought.

But, wait! Something was coming. The figure leant forward to look towards Birling Gap. The third ciggie was flicked away half-smoked and the figure moved silently round to the front end of the car, bending down to engage the attention of whoever was occupying the car's front seats.

Twisting slightly in his wheelchair Ben followed the figure's gaze. With the aid of his binoculars, he could make out a set of weak headlights distantly blinking along the twisting road. As the apparition drew nearer, he heard the thin rattle of its engine.

At length it came into view. It braked, then crunched cautiously over the road and drew to a stop in the lay-by below him, a few yards along from the police car. It too turned off lights and engine. Ben, aware that Snuff's snoring was only too audible, gently shook the dog into consciousness.

The vehicle was small, a rectangular shape. A van?

Ben watched intently. The dog, sensing a new tension, sat up, fixing his eyes on him and waiting for some indication of what was going to happen.

Yet nothing seemed to call for any action. Down below it was as if the occupants of each vehicle had no knowledge of the others. And without the glow of the cigarette to guide him Ben could not even make out the silent figure. Had it moved along to the van? He had a sense of movement but could see or hear nothing. It seemed that, like actors on a darkened stage waiting for the curtain to rise, they were all waiting for a cue.

Several minutes passed. Then he heard noises which subsequently he was to try to describe many times to many different people. A muffled sequence of sounds. Like a pile of cardboard boxes tumbling haphazardly on to a wooden floor, was how Ben later described it. Snuff heard it too, but equally ignorant of the source, looked hopefully about him, waiting for enlightenment.

It was only a flicker in the shadows, but Ben had a sense of movement, some new activity taking place, silently, in the darkness below him.

Then, without warning, the police car's engine purred into sudden life and the vehicle pulled smoothly away, its bright rear lights tracing its progress along the country road towards Birling Gap, until it was swallowed by the night. After no more than a couple of minutes, the van likewise crackled into life, tortuously executed a gear-crunching three-point turn and rattled off in the same direction.

Leaving only the black shroud of night, which has throughout history covered so many crimes.

As it had covered this one.

* * *

On the same evening that Ben and Snuff kept their lonely vigil on Beachy Head, Ben's wife Julia was upstairs in a trim little maisonette in Eastbourne's Old Town, lying naked by her younger lover. She was smiling contentedly across at him, willing him not to interrogate her on how she had judged his performance.

It was not that this had been unsatisfactory - far from it. Physically, they were perfectly matched. The only downside was that her sexual partner tended to regard lovemaking as a kind of athletic display, of which Julia was the field judge. It was good that right from the start he had taken all the false sentiment out of what was still – though her husband knew all about these sessions – an act of adultery. Yet it was depressing that, like a toddler being potty-trained, he wanted to be praised for performing what was after all a perfectly natural act. Which was not to deny that he had performed it well. It was just that now, during what should have been comfortable post-coital relaxation, he would want to know how he had been assessed and therefore what position he now occupied in the roster of Julia's lovers.

For the moment he was lying on his back, where they had rolled apart, beads of sweat still adhering to the dark hairs on his chest. But even as she looked he propped himself up on his elbows and turned towards her, the inevitable question already forming on his lips.

She forestalled him. "That was lovely. I can't think why Helen ever left you."

"Well, she did."

"You talk about her a lot. Do you still miss her?"

"Of course not. Why don't you move in with me?"

"Don't be silly." Shuffling across to the edge of the bed, she reached for her underclothes. "Why would I do that?"

"Do you discuss me?" After a few seconds, more insistently, "Well, do you talk about me? Do you?"

"You know our arrangement. What is there to discuss?"

"I'm being used."

Now Julia was searching for her lipstick. "Isn't that what you want? To be used?"

"By you, yes. Not by him."

She was saved by the pinging of her mobile.

Briskly, "Julia Jackson-Grant. Assistant Commissioner, Police and Law." Her voice softened, "Yes. I'm on my way. Oh, have you? That sounds promising. Just give me a few minutes." She mouthed 'Husband' at her paramour.

He was robing himself in a purple dressing gown, tying the belt with a petulant frown.

"Why is he calling you now?"

"There's no cause to worry, my sweet."

She drew up her sharply-creased trousers and pulled on her yellow gilet. From her cosmetic bag she took out a sealed white envelope and placed it on the dressing table.

"Thanks."

"You've earned it tonight."

"I'm yours to command."

"True." Saying which she smiled her enigmatic smile, descended the stairs and paused in the tiny hallway to pull on her coat and wrap her Paisley scarf about her neck. "I'll ring you," Julia said to the figure coming down the stairs, "at the usual time."

She shut the door behind her and walked briskly down the deserted street to where she had parked the blue people carrier. She performed the quick searches which were required of her every time she got into a vehicle. Then climbed in, checked her pistol was still securely in place in the glove compartment and revved up the engine, before heading out along the lonely road to Beachy Head.

The landscape on either side of her was black and featureless, with the faintest trace of sea mist as she wound her way along the familiar road. There was no other traffic. She switched the headlights up to full, so the beams raked over the closely-cropped grass and from time to time exposed a huddled group of sheep, jostling coyly in the headlights' glare, like boarding school girls caught smoking after lights out.

She slowed down as she approached the lay-by where she would make contact with her husband.

She was almost upon it before she saw the body. It had been roughly arranged against the dusty stone wall that fringed the lay-by, its head lolling obscenely, blood glinting darkly around the hole in the middle of its shattered face.

The car juddered to a stop.

She sat quite still for a moment. Then, gingerly, she got out and took two or three tentative steps towards the corpse, holding her breath so she should not smell the vile matter oozing from it.

Three black rooks rose from the wall from which they had been surveying their carrion flesh and flew angrily away over the farmland.

A gust of wind stirred a hank of its matted hair.

The one thing clearly apparent was that this faceless heap of flesh and blood-sodden clothing was the mutilated body of a uniformed police officer.

* * *

As Ben and Snuff kept their lonely vigil Clifford Mollison, of *Mollison and Craxton; Solicitors*, having no pressing work on hand, had enjoyed a lads-only session at the pub at East Dean with a group of chaps from the local Chamber of Commerce. In his younger days he had invariably been the life and soul of any party, whether as host or guest, and he hung grimly on to his reputation as a man who worked hard and played hard - though nowadays he did neither of these things. Last night as usual he'd been careful to maintain the impression that he was still a bit of a lad. He had made a great deal of noise to cover the fact he was drinking sparingly and had taken a walk around the village ostensibly to 'clear his head' but actually to buy time. Later, he had swayed about slightly and slurred his words as the landlord, a stickler for timekeeping, uttered the traditional incantation: "Drink up now; have you no homes to go to?"

Mollison had a home to go to, and his wife Gwen - big, fiercely bespectacled and cocooned in a glossy black plastic coat - was waiting in her Renault to convey him to it. Gwen was quite a big fish in Eastbourne's social pond. Her need to undertake any form of paid work had ended when she married the affluent Clifford and, after a few years of careful social climbing, had been admitted to that elite corps of well-to-do 'volunteers' who in Eastbourne ran such things as the charity shops, fun-runs and hospital radio.

She started off as soon as Cliff had assumed the passenger seat, flash-freezing his ebullient mood with her glacial disapproval. Nor did they break the silence when they arrived home. In order to maintain his pretence of discreet hellraising, Clifford drank three glasses of cold water in their expensively laid-out kitchen before they passed upstairs and, from opposite sides, climbed into their king-sized bed.

Clifford slept fitfully. When his ringtone shrieked out at five to one the following morning, its clatter mingled alarmingly with a nightmare in which he was lying under a tarpaulin, hiding from a posse of shrieking harpies circling his refuge with glinting rapiers.

"For the love of Mary, stop that bloody row," his lady wife commanded from beneath the duvet. He groped for his mobile on his bedside table and drew it myopically

JOHN PICK

towards him. Obstinately, it carried on ringing. "Cut them off, for God's sake," came the muffled order.

"I can't, it's Julia." Mollison stood uncertainly, momentarily catching sight of himself in the long dressing mirror; a middle-aged and slightly clownish figure, hair protruding at unusual angles, with his mouth devoid of its daytime dentures and hanging apishly open. He turned away from this unlovely spectacle and clamped the mobile to his ear. "Sorry, Julia. Could you say that again?"

Ignoring the muffled commentary from the bed, he pulled on his horn-rimmed spectacles and gave his full attention to the mobile, screwing up his features and unwittingly reproducing the Michael Gove impression that had, on the previous evening, been such a hit with the Chamber of Commerce gang. "What, now? OK. I'll be there in twenty minutes. Sooner if I can."

"I've got to go out," he told the duvet. "A situation has developed."

Soothed by his adoption of solicitor's jargon, he began to assemble his daytime self. A few minutes later, hair brushed, dental plates in position, mouth cleansed by a slurp of mouthwash, clean shirt and tie and a suitably sober three-piece suit hanging on his lean frame, he was able to bid a curt farewell to the sullen bedclothes, "I'm not sure what time I'll be back."

Fifteen minutes after that, he was taking in the scene in the lay-by. The corpse slouched in the glare of the

12

floodlights, with screens being erected around it. White-clad figures unloading boxes and coils of wire from the Incident Van. A group of officers marking out the lay-by with white tape, apparently preparing to do an inch-by-inch search. One of their number, with face mask and rubber gloves in place, had the unappetising task of pulling out and itemising the contents of a nearby litter bin.

Standing by her car was the tall, shapely figure of Julia. Nearby, he noticed with mild surprise, was her husband Ben, with that insanitary old dog of his stretched out on his lap. He was talking to a small group of top police brass – the one they called Plod and two others that Clifford recognised only by sight.

Julia strode straight over and began talking before he had properly levered himself out of the Jag. "Thank you for coming. I was first on the scene, so I shall have to make a statement." Not for the first time, he noticed that when Julia spoke, nothing in her elegant features moved except for her lips. "I don't want there to be any misunderstanding, so I thought it best to have my solicitor with me."

* * *

Preliminary Statement of Julia Jackson-Grant. [November 30th. 3.05 a.m.]

On the mid-evening of November 29th I dropped off my husband, Ben Jackson-Grant, at a lay-by on the coastal road, near Birling Gap. Having lowered his motorised wheelchair on to the lay-by, I then helped him find a suitable 'hide' from which he could observe and log the night life of the birds on Beachy Head. Birding is a hobby of his. Having made sure he was comfortable, and had his equipment and suitable hot drinks, I arranged to pick him up later, together with his dog.

At about 12.30 I received a call from him saying he had recorded everything of interest and asking me to pick him up as arranged. A few minutes later I got in to my people carrier (which is adapted for the wheelchair) and drove up to the place where I had left him. As I approached the agreed location I saw what at first I thought might be a children's guy which had been dumped there after Fireworks Night, but as I neared it I saw that it was the mutilated body of a police officer, which had been propped up against the wall of the lay-by.

I immediately stopped the people carrier, got out and phoned the police. In the short time before they arrived I walked up the grassy bank and helped navigate my husband down to the road level, by which time the first police car was arriving. My husband will tell you that he had no foreknowledge of the ghastly sight which awaited him down here on the roadway.

I have given this statement voluntarily and shall be happy to assist with further information at any future date, if requested.

Julia Jackson-Grant [S. E. Area Asst. P&L Commissioner]
Witnessed; Clifford Mollison, Solicitor
Inspector P. Plover

Preliminary Statement of Detective Inspector Ben Grant
(Retd.) [November 30th. 3.20 p.m.]

*Since my accident and subsequent retirement from the
Force I have become more involved in bird watching
and am, together with other local enthusiasts, preparing
a short pamphlet on bird life on the Downs.*

*On November 29th I asked my wife Julia to drive me
up here above Beachy Head at around 20.30 hours,
then to help manoeuvre me into a suitable hide from
which I could view and record bird life. This she did,
arranging to pick me up when I had finished.*

*While occupied with my hobby, I was aware of very
little activity on the Birling Gap road. I watched a
police car pull in to the lay-by around half past ten and
stay for perhaps ten minutes. One or two cars went
by, and I think one of these may also have spent a
little time in the lay-by. I took little notice of this, being
preoccupied with my own concerns. I also heard
nothing unexpected, except for an irregular thumping
noise around a quarter to eleven, as if someone nearby
was unloading and dumping crates from the back of
a lorry.*

*This morning, my work being complete, at around
00.30 hrs, I telephoned Julia, who came to help me
down the slope and into her car. When she arrived at my
makeshift hide, she was in a state of some agitation.
She informed me of what she had seen and told me that
she had already phoned for the police. After I had
regained the road I saw the body. Neither my wife nor*

I approached the crime scene nor otherwise interfered with it.

I have given this statement voluntarily and should be happy to supply any further information pertinent to this case.

Detective Inspector Ben Jackson- Grant (Retd.)
Witnessed; Clifford Mollison, Solicitor
Inspector P. Plover

* * *

To the scorn of his lady wife, the following morning Clifford slept in and didn't set out for his office until after one o' clock. His secretary Miss Foster had left a list of missed calls including, he saw, one marked 'Most Urgent'. It was from Julia.

She picked up straight away. "Clifford, I called you several times. Your secretary said you weren't in the office. Where were you?"

"Catching up on my beauty sleep."

"When can I see you? Something important has happened."

"I have clients at two and three. Can I see you after that?"

"Four o' clock then. And Ben will join us."

He's like a paid companion who speaks only when spoken to. It's clear who wears the trousers in that house, Clifford thought.

"Will do." He said and put down the receiver. Almost immediately the tiny red light on his desk phone started to wink. It would most likely be one of the Chamber of Commerce chaps to whom he had given his personal work number.

It was. Unfortunately, it was Dick Rodham, an unimportant member of the Chamber who earned his living, or so he claimed, from a small independent Estate Agency in nearby Newhaven. His fellow professionals regarded him as being a bit of a chancer, not the sort of bloke you'd buy a used apartment from. In his dealings with his business chums however Dick was determinedly, annoyingly, affable.

"Cliff! Where were you all morning, man?"

"Sleeping."

"Sleeping! Well, I had a bit of a head first thing, I must admit. But I took a couple of alkies and downed a pot of black coffee. Then I was right as rain! Raring to go! In the office by nine o' clock. You're losing your touch, boyo."

"I was up most of the night. Called out. On a case."

"Oh! All is forgiven then." Rodham's tone suddenly became serious. "That business on Beachy Head, was it? Poor sod was a copper from down here in Newhaven, apparently. What happened?"

"I can't talk about it now, Dick."

"Of course not, matey. See you in Lodge Thursday night, shall we?"

"I can't talk about it then, either."

"Quite understand. Secret stuff. Russians involved. Wheels within wheels." Upon which, having exhausted his stock of laddish banter, Rodham said well he had work to do, even if Clifford didn't and rang off in that irritating way he had, yapping repetitively, 'Bye, bye, bye' his voice getting fainter and fainter, as if he just thrown himself off a cliff. "If only," Clifford murmured, to nobody in particular.

Though Rodham had spoken no more than the truth. Mollison indeed had no work to do that day – no office work at any rate. The appointments he had mentioned to Julia were a fabrication, arising partly from his small-town businessman's instinct to seem busier than he was, and partly because he needed time to mull over the events of the previous night. For the inescapable fact was that Clifford had grown idle and was nowadays more interested in giving the appearance of being a businessman than in doing any business.

For long periods he stared vacantly out of his office windows at Eastbourne's hard-working citizens going about their affairs. He encouraged others to diligent labour but for himself was perfectly happy doing nothing. In his capacious office nobody disturbed him – certainly not his secretary, who had in any case gone out shopping. At three thirty, he drank the tea and swallowed the indigestion pill a junior brought him.

At ten minutes to four he set out for Ben and Julia's well-guarded pad on the edge of Lewes.

In their drawing room the lights were on and the curtains already drawn against the approaching night. In the grate one bar of a cheap electric fire glowed dimly. Clifford glanced hopefully at the decanters set out on a shadowy side table, but Julia was already into her stride.

"You will readily appreciate," she was saying, "that Ben and I have been placed in an awkward position. Clifford, we need your advice. Go on, Ben."

"Last night, up on Beachy Head, I wasn't just looking at birds," Ben's voice, as befitted one used to giving police evidence in Magistrates' Courts, was flat and undramatic. "I was, in point of fact, keeping a lookout."

"A lookout? For what?"

"What we are about to tell you," cut in Julia, "must go no further. I must have that understood." Clifford nodded and made a curious downward motion with his arms to indicate that he was after all their solicitor and could be implicitly trusted.

"I had been given the information that some kind of drug cartel was operating along the south coast and that senior police officers from this area were involved. Probably all nonsense. My source told me that the group were going to make a drop up there in the lay-by around eleven last night. It all sounded like fantasy but you'll appreciate that in my position I have to take these things seriously. And because of the nature of the allegation I couldn't very well involve the local police force."

"So, you asked Ben to …?"

Julia nodded. "Just in case there was something in it."

"And there was." He frowned.

From the corner of his eye Mollison saw a long shape detach itself from the room's shadows and waddle importantly over to Ben, who indulgently tickled the canine's ear. "Snuff shared my vigil, didn't you, boy?"

He's going senile Mollison thought. Looking from one to the other he wondered, not for the first time, how the three of them managed to live together under one roof. As someone with experience of domestic disharmony, he found each of the three, for quite separate reasons, impossible to conceive of as a companion. Word in Sussex was that underneath her cool exterior Julia was quite a woman. Unkind friends said that during her years at Girton she had not lost her public-school mannerisms, but she had lost everything else. Her time in the City had been punctuated by a string of affairs then, after her marriage to Harry Jackson, it was said she'd climbed the social ladder in the South East by means of some astute bed-hopping, so nobody was surprised when she was named the guilty party in their divorce. But she carried it all off with considerable chutzpah, did very well out of it financially and had bought the large property in Lewes out of the proceeds. She had then surprised her circle by marrying beneath her - albeit to the sharpest copper in the South East. Though her new husband had not been without his faults. Since his accident the sins of the flesh to which he had formerly been prone had given way to irritation and bouts of melancholy. And as for that bloody dog, mindlessly slavering on the hearthrug, it should be put down. Didn't each of them realise the other two were grossly unsuitable?

Aloud he said, "You must add this information to your previous statements."

"Clifford," Ben said with a sudden urgency, "It's more serious than that. The body in the lay-by was P.C. Fletcher, right? From Newhaven?"

"Surely you're not telling me you had anything to do with..."

"That's exactly what I am telling you." He shifted in his wheelchair and faced Clifford full on. "It was Fletcher, see, who was the whistle blower. It was P.C. Fletcher who passed on the information to Julia."

Mollison in his excitement adopted the language of a Chicago cop, "So, you're telling me this guy Fletcher was silenced to keep his mouth shut?"

Julia nodded grimly, "What else are we to think? They must have known that Fletcher had been talking. And they must have known Ben was up there. And they must have known that I'd find the body when I picked up Ben."

Her sharp voice tinkled on, with Ben nodding metronomically. "Inspector Plover is coming here tonight to give me a heads-up on the case. I asked him to. It's bound to be a big story in the press - 'Assistant Commissioner in Murder Mystery', kind of thing." She shuddered before adding grimly, "We must tell him about Fletcher, mustn't we?"

"Yes. With your Solicitor present of course. I advise you both to expand your statements."

Ben nodded his agreement. "Well - no time like the present."

Mollison clicked open his laptop.

* * *

After Julia had departed, her lover had smoked a joint and put a few things in the wash before climbing back upstairs, carrying a sliver of script with 'Kenneth Molloy' stamped across it. He picked up the envelope which Julia had left, counted its contents approvingly, then seated himself on the ruffled bed, put on his horn-rimmed spectacles and stared blankly at the few pages which contained Inspector Bull's speeches.

He found it difficult to concentrate. Although, truth to tell, the part he was studying did not demand urgent attention. Inspector Bull was a small supporting role in a televised soap opera in which one of the leading characters, played by a notorious old Thespian lecher, was due to meet an untimely end at the hands of his glamorous blonde wife. The latter part was taken by a supposedly much-loved but permanently inebriated actress, who was slated to be sensationally tried for murder over the coming episodes. The producers however knew that, whatever the jury's verdict, she was going to be shunted out of the soap. But, before that unpleasantness hit the fan, viewers would see a highly dramatic trial at which, Kenneth hoped, Inspector Bull would again make an appearance.

Jobbing actors had to consider these things.

When he'd first left Drama School he'd thought, with his matinee idol looks and home counties voice, that he stood a good chance of becoming a leading man. His partner Helen, who had graduated from the same establishment, had repeatedly told him that was where his destiny lay. But that had not happened. Indeed, it was Helen who had begun to climb the theatrical ladder. So much so that when his mother had died two years previously and he had inherited the bijou Eastbourne property, Kenneth found it difficult to persuade her that they should move down to the Sunshine Coast together and set up house. Eastbourne was, in the eyes of an ambitious young actress, spiritually and geographically a very long way from the West End. With the result that, after vacillating for some weeks, Helen decided that the demands of her career meant that she must again take up residence in London. They had agreed that they would keep in touch, although both knew that in their business it was unlikely to happen. So, Helen left Kenneth behind in genteel Eastbourne and moved in to a flat in Kilburn with a girl-friend (who also described herself as an actor, though she was for the time-being earning a crust in a Cricklewood Estate Agency).

Helen's departure meant that Kenneth's life now contained two gaping lacunae. First was the fact that her going had left him bereft of a sexual companion - and sex played an important part of Kenneth's life. The second was that although he would continue to be offered supporting roles on television, and occasionally asked to join cheap stage tours, without Helen's contributions to the budget the household income was too low to fund the kind of life he thought he deserved. Keeping up appearances, even in Eastbourne, still demanded a lot of scrimping and saving.

It might all have ended in disaster, had Kenneth not had a one-night stand with Soozie, a middle-aged lady of colour who kept house for her father in Langney, in the East end of the town. That came about at a particularly low point in his theatrical career. A few months after Helen's departure, penury had forced Kenneth to accept a temporary job as a shelf-stacker in a local supermarket. He did this lowly job without complaint but took no account of his fellow-workers, fastidiously refusing to mingle with people from whom a serious artiste such as himself could surely draw no benefit. That was before Soozie - a supervisor of till staff - had taken a shine to Kenneth's virile, well-groomed appearance. One Tuesday morning, as they smoked a joint during their mid-morning break, she had quietly suggested that they might enjoy a night together between the sheets. She came with no baggage, she said, adding that all she wanted was a good seeing-to. Was he up for it?

Soozie was not Kenneth's usual style. A cheerful forty-something with tumbling black ringlets, a formidable posterior and an emphatic pointy bust, she was the kind of woman Kenneth's mother would certainly have labelled 'common'. But her earthiness awakened something in Kenneth. He was definitely up for it.

They met on the following Saturday and the fixture proved an undoubted success. Soozie was refreshingly free of inhibition and noisily enjoyed their athletic couplings. For his part Kenneth had not until then realised how much he had been missing such carnal delights - nor how much he had missed the frank intimacies of pillow talk during which personal hang-ups could be whispered and consolation offered.

Most of all, their Saturday night coupling flattered Kenneth's vanity because Soozie, who had by her own admission been round the block a few times, rated his performance highly. And Kenneth cherished good notices, even when they were given for work in this unconventional arena. Moreover, her assessment had a further consequence which became clear the following morning.

The two of them were chatting over a leisurely breakfast, when Soozie casually suggested that Kenneth could solve both of his outstanding problems by promoting himself in the area as a high-class gigolo. Now Helen had departed it would be the means of gaining both the sexual fulfilment and the larger income he said he lacked.

Kenneth took this as harmless banter. But no, Soozie insisted she was perfectly serious. Eastbourne, she informed him matter-of-factly, already had a lively swinging scene and it was full of rich widows who were, in Soozie's unlovely phrase, 'gagging for it'. "And you're good at it, Kenneth. You've got the equipment. We must each make best use of what talents we got."

With an embarrassed gesture of dismissal, "No, no, apart from anything else I wouldn't know how to set it all up. Or what to – "

"To wear? Just a swanky bathrobe. I'll loan you mine," referring to the startlingly purple one carelessly belted around her generous midriff.

"Or what to charge? Oh, leave that to your ladies. They'll pay you what you're worth." She wagged a plump finger at him, "which is plenty." She chuckled knowingly. "But it was my idea, so I'm telling you, I shall want a cut of the profits."

Humouring her, "Where do gigolos advertise? Not in the *Herald*, surely?"

"There's always *Friday Ad*. But you shouldn't advertise with the prozzies. Be classy. Go on the web. Or put it in one of the classy mags like *Horse and Hound*." She giggled. "Hard-working rider for generous fillies. Age no barrier. Eastbourne area."

"I couldn't put myself up for …"

"Don't you like doing it then? Were you pretending?" She moved around to his chair, reached down and felt for his member. "I know plenty of women who'd pay for this."

A few moments later. "Kenneth my boy! It seems to me like you're beginning to like the idea." Still smiling, she bent down over his lap.

Then she stopped talking.

Thus it was, in the course of a Sunday morning blow job, that the possibility of a second career as a professional sex worker began to take root in Kenneth's mind. Which career, by various twists and turns of fate, meant that only a few months later he would be sharing a bed of lust with Julia Jackson-Grant.

* * *

Inspector Plover was well aware of his unflattering soubriquet, even if none of his young colleagues dared to call him 'P.C. Plod' to his face. His older companions however were a different kettle of fish. Long acquaintanceship had given them the right to use his nickname (out of hearing of the junior staff). They used it always with a light salting of irony, as 'Plod' suggested heavy conformity and the Plover they knew was hard-working, quick-witted and, incidentally, gay.

He was not one to stand on his dignity. Although he had not slept for nearly twenty hours, Plover had mutely accepted the Area Deputy's request that he give her an account of all that had happened since the discovery of Fletcher's body. And he'd agreed to her request that he attend her in her own home.

As he was crunching up the Jackson-Grants' short drive in the early evening, the light from the French windows showed his old boss's wheelchair parked on the lawn with its occupant presiding over his hound's toilet. He lowered his car window and called out a greeting. Ben waved and called, "Hi, Plod," adding, "Julia's waiting for you," with a gesture showing that Julia was waiting in the house and was not, as Plod might otherwise have thought, crouched in the shrubbery ready to spring on him.

There was an unfamiliar car parked in front of Julia's double garage, by the side of the People Carrier, so he left his own on the drive. He yawned discreetly as he shuffled over the gravel and trudged up the ramp to the back door. Where, despite his repeated ringing of the bell, his presence went unheeded.

Until he felt what seemed like a roll of carpet wriggle its way between his legs to the doorstep. Snuff, realising this lumbering biped did not understand even the simplest of household routines, took the necessary action. He emitted a raw phlegmy yelp, not unlike the flushing of a cruise ship toilet. This got immediate results. From the garden Ben shouted that he was coming, hold on, and at the same time the back door opened to reveal Julia, a mobile phone clamped to her ear. "Oh, you mustn't be without. I'll get him to bring you some over," she said to it before clicking the instrument off and standing back to allow first Snuff, then Plover, to come inside.

Once ensconced within, Plover submitted placidly to being asked to wait in the unheated corridor, watching the dog in the kitchen being fed what looked like rare steak. He then had to push himself flat against the wall to allow Ben's motorised wheelchair to go past and stand aside again as a replete Snuff padded by, following his master into the tiny study at the far end of the corridor, the door of which shut decisively.

At length Julia emerged, greeting Plover with a furrowed brow as if he were a thoughtless neighbour who had called at an inconvenient moment, rather than someone who was there by her specific invitation. "We'll talk in the lounge," she said.

Which room, Plover noted on arrival, already contained Clifford Mollison.

Julia did not offer a detailed explanation for the solicitor's presence, merely announcing that everything that was going to be said would be said in absolute confidence.

She asked Plover to set out what developments there had been so far.

He went methodically through his first-day report. Fletcher had been killed with a shot to the head and thereafter somebody had brutally attacked the skull in an apparent attempt to obliterate his features. They were working on the autopsy but no results would appear until the following day. Meanwhile the on-site search had revealed no bullets or gunpowder in the immediate vicinity, and it was therefore possible that Fletcher had been killed elsewhere and the body brought to the lay-by. The police car deployed in the incident had been recovered from the car park in East Dean, still in pristine condition. But where exactly the murder and disfigurement had taken place was so far unknown.

It appeared there had been nothing remarkable about Fletcher's working day. He'd done his shift driving a patrol car finishing, as scheduled, at 19.00 hours. He'd signed out as usual. Though there was one thing that didn't make a lot of sense. As Julia had seen for herself when she'd discovered the body - at the time of his murder Fletcher was still wearing his uniform. So, Plover concluded, the first question to ask was why did Fletcher keep his uniform on after work? Secondly, where did he die, and over and above everything else, what had he done to deserve such diabolical treatment?

"These are the questions we need to answer, ma'am." Plover fell silent and waited for comment.

Julia was normally very free with speculation and advice, but this time she had nothing to offer. Instead she looked sharply over at Mollison who coughed significantly and leaned forward in his chair. "Before we go any further, Mrs Jackson-Grant would like to make a statement."

Without preamble Julia told them that as Deputy Area Commissioner it was her policy to make herself available to all ranks. So, when a week or so ago PC Fletcher had asked to see her for an off-the-record talk she had agreed. What he had told her – that he'd learned there was a drug-running gang operating on the South Coast, and that members of the Police Force were involved – had of course sounded fanciful, but she'd agreed to look into it. When he'd added that there was going to be a drop in the lay-by up on Beachy Head, and that a police car would be involved, she had asked her husband to keep watch, as in the circumstances she could not ask the serving police. That was the reason Ben was up there last night. She had not of course realised when she first came upon it that the faceless corpse was that of her informant, Fletcher. As soon as she learned that it was, she had rung her solicitor and when he was able to attend to the matter that afternoon, she and Ben had amended their statements.

It was a moment before Plover spoke.

"Who else has this information?"

"Just we three, and Ben."

"And, we must presume, Keith Fletcher's killer?"

Having posed the question, Plover fell silent again. A few moments later Julia, having unburdened herself of her personal story, felt it incumbent upon her to press on with her theories.

31

"Surely it is safe to assume that it was the drug gang that killed Fletcher?" Mollison lent emphasis to her words by nodding.

"If Fletcher was telling you the truth, ma'am. But we must not presume that he was. Tell me," Plover went on, "Have you, or Ben, left the house today?"

"No, we haven't."

"Apart from Mr Mollison and me, has anyone visited you?"

"No."

"Have you phoned anyone? Answered the phone?"

"Naturally we've answered the phone. The newshounds have been on to me all day, but I'm quite used to stonewalling them. And if you are suggesting that I've discussed what PC Fletcher told me with anybody else, then you insult my integrity. Even when I recruited my own husband to keep watch, I told him only what he needed to know."

"You've told him the full story now?"

"Naturally, as soon as I knew that the body was Fletcher. And I immediately tried to get in touch with my solicitor," with a sharp look at that functionary, "but as I told you he wasn't available until late this afternoon."

"As soon as I heard the details," said Mollison, "I advised my clients to enlarge their statements."

"Quite right," murmured Plover, "Quite right."

"Inspector, you're tired out," said Julia. "Go home to bed."

He did not demur.

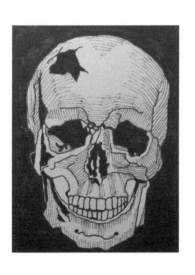

TWO

The following morning Plover was at his desk early. By ten thirty he had spoken to the top brass, cleared his diary for the next six weeks, finalised the small team that was going to assist him and made it clear to everybody else that he would not give his name to anything but the blandest possible press release until enquiries were further advanced. Julia and Ben's expanded statements he had, for the moment, locked away in a drawer, also pending further enquiries.

Britain's national press did not share Plover's respect for facts. The front pages of the morning editions were filled with wild speculation about what the murder of the Newhaven police officer portended, while radio and television programmes had drawn upon their seemingly inexhaustible supply of expert commentators to debate the immediate causes of the murder. They asked themselves penetratingly whether it should simply be blamed on government cutbacks or whether it was the harbinger of riots, of the breakdown of Western society or of a full-blown nuclear war. For some of the red tops it was a clear signal that the UK police should be armed; for others it showed that patriotic Englishmen were right to demand the return of the rope.

Meanwhile, behind his uncluttered desk Plover was striving to keep calm in the face of the sullen truculence of the young man facing him. "Come on, lad," he urged the interviewee. "You must have noticed something that would help us."

"But there wasn't nothing to notice, sir. He was just an ordinary bloke. Came out with the lads sometimes. Liked a beer."

"Girl friend? Boy Friend?"

"Don't know sir, never saw neither."

"Bit of a loner, then?"

"In a way." By way of explanation, "He went to the library. In Grove Road."

"I know where the library is. Ok - so what kind of books did he read?"

"Don't know, sir."

"Do you know where Fletcher came from? Don't know that either? Well, I'll tell you."

Plover had the Southerner's inbred suspicion of the North. "He came from Sheffield," he said with the air of someone revealing that a popular local priest was also a practising cannibal, "From Sheffield! Now can you see why he was so pleased to be posted down here?"

"No, sir, not really."

"No? Look around you lad. If you'd been born in Sheffield wouldn't you be thrilled to be posted to East Sussex? Do you know the crime figures for South Yorkshire?"

"No, sir."

A confident rap on the door, and they were interrupted by Plover's number two, a red-faced, well-rounded middle-aged Sergeant who was known throughout the force by his surname, Harris. He was addressed as such even by his wife and grown-up daughter. Today, wearing his usual baleful expression, he glanced in passing at the young man and deposited a thin sheaf of papers on Plover's desk. He received in return a wry glance from his chief, followed by an open-arm shrug, like a bored umpire signalling a wide. Harris nodded vigorously towards the papers, following which Plover made an unequivocal 'beat it' sign to the youth, who scuttled gratefully out of the room.

As soon as the door had shut, they reverted to speech. "Jackson-Grant was a member of the East Sussex Ornithological Society, sir. Been a member for three years, apparently. And they are producing a booklet on bird life on the Seven Sisters." He sat down heavily. "Went to see the Secretary first thing up Alfriston way. Military type. Made me put my identification through his letter box. Surprising old cove." Harris screwed up his features in an unavailing attempt to recall what had particularly surprised him about the said cove.

"That's one in a thousand," said Plover, without making it clear to which one he was referring.

Then, plucking a printout from the papers Harris had given him, "What's this?"

"List of Fletcher's personal effects. We've been through his room in Newhaven."

Plover ran his eyes down it and grunted.

"Nothing here. No fags. No booze bill from the offie. No porn. No drugs. Too good to be true. What's this OU receipt then?"

"Open University. Fletcher was studying Moral Philosophy." Harris made it sound like a sexual perversion.

"Good God! Man's a saint. Why in heaven's name should anyone want to kill him? I just don't see what the motive could have been." Harris shook his head in sympathy until, feeling it incumbent on him to contribute something to the discussion, he dug out a phrase from his repertoire of truisms. "Only time will tell, sir," he said heavily, "Only time will – "

Plover, who did not value Harris for his conversation, cut brusquely in:

"Murder team meeting. In here. Today. 2 0' Clock sharp."

* * *

Colonel Baxter's routine had been disturbed twice that morning. First was breakfast time TV which had carried news of the South Downs murder. The report began tastelessly but inevitably with a smiling picture of P.C. Fletcher. This was followed in its turn by a brief shot of the Beachy Head cliff top which panned to the police tent covering the lay-by, its white canvas faintly agitated by the coastal wind. The piece was rounded off by a clip of Inspector Plover coming out of a big stone porchway and waving away reporters, accompanied by a solemn voice-over which said that the police were anxious to contact anybody with any information about these events.

The contrast between the dead man's smiling face and the chilly desolation of the crime scene was so great that the Colonel, who did not in the normal way consider himself an emotional man, found himself shedding tears at the pity of it all.

The second thing was the unexpected arrival of Harris. The doorbell chimed just after nine o' clock to reveal his bulky form. He arrived in an unmarked car and wore a grey mac over his uniform in order not to alarm either the Colonel or his neighbours - a ruse which unfortunately backfired. The Colonel, whose military career had been topped off with a short spell as a Neighbourhood Constable, wanted Harris to identify himself properly, and insisted he post his identification through the letter box. Negotiation over this procedure took a good ten minutes. When he had granted him admission Baxter made the Sergeant take off his shoes before entering the dining room, leaving him standing in Mrs Harris's thick knitted socks while Baxter rummaged in an upstairs cupboard for the membership and subscription lists. Answering the questions about Ben Grant's membership of the Ornithological Society had taken up another fifteen minutes, questions about the upcoming publications another twenty. The upshot of all this was that Baxter had been forced to delay his daily walk in to Alfriston and had moreover missed his regular 'elevenses' - milky coffee and blueberry muffin at the Cat's Cradle Tea Shoppe in the High Street.

Truth to tell, Harris's appearance had rattled the Colonel. He did not in any case take kindly to unannounced visits and he suspected the Sergeant's reason for calling. It was not until Baxter had point-blank refused to let him see the members' names and addresses without disclosing his motives that Harris had been forced to admit his enquiries were in connection with the murder of young Fletcher. An indignant Baxter had then insisted he should be told what his birdwatchers had to do with this brutal killing, but Harris would not be drawn further. He would only say that they didn't yet have a suspect. In the initial stages, he said, it was more a matter of ruling people out of their enquiries.

After the Sergeant had departed, Baxter was overcome with a yearning for intelligent company, for somebody with whom he could discuss these sensational matters. He even caught himself wishing that it could have been one of the two mornings a week that his housekeeper Mrs Tomkins wobbled up on her bicycle and did for him. Then he could have discussed it all with her and told her the theories already forming in his mind as to the probable identity of the killer. But it was not one of Mrs Tomkins' mornings. So, the Colonel pulled himself together and started his preparations to go forth in quest of another audience.

But, what with one thing and another, it was nearly noon when Baxter, arms held stiffly by his side like an Irish dancer, marched down Alfriston High Street and turned into his usual lunchtime pub. He unwound his dark blue muffler as he entered, piggy eyes adjusting slowly to the darkness within. He looked about for intelligent listeners in the thinly populated room, rejecting Gretchen the barmaid on account of her sex, and the scattered groups of office workers on account of their social inferiority. Then his eye lighted on a lone young man sitting along from the open fire who was, incredibly for these parts, actually reading a book. Like a homing missile Baxter moved towards him, steering a direct course across the bar room floor, dislodging chairs and sending bar stools spinning in the process.

Alerted by the commotion, the young man looked up.

"Don't mind if I join ya, d'ya?"

There did not seem to be a choice. As the Colonel hung his duffel coat on the back of his chair, the young man looked wistfully past him to the empty chairs arranged about the room and murmured that he hoped his new companion wouldn't mind if he went on with his book.

"Reading, are we?" said the Colonel at a volume which made it sound as if he were demonstrating on a training film how infiltrators could strike up conversations behind enemy lines without drawing attention to themselves, if only they knew the lingo. "What's that ya reading, eh?"

Warily, the young man showed him.

"Well, you surprise me! I shouldn't have thought y'were that type. Glad to see it though. What makes y' interested in his stuff?"

Baxter never received an answer. For even as he posed the question a figure had entered the bar behind him. This entity evidently posed some sort of a challenge to the young man who stared crossly over the Colonel's shoulder, emitted a brief groan, closed his book then bent low as he stuffed it into his canvas bag, muttering softly to himself.

"Too many, too many." He stood and pushed clumsily past the Colonel, "Too many cooks." And in a curious crab-like scuttle, face averted from the bar, he clattered out on to the street. Baxter caught a last glimpse of him scurrying towards the Green.

The young man's nemesis, a woman, was now ordering a drink at the bar. At first glance she looked like an unremarkable, heavily-upholstered lady of middle age, wearing a beret on her almost perfectly spherical head and substantial suede boots on her feet. Between these extremities a generously proportioned sheepskin jacket encircled her form. As she had untoggled the upper part of this it was possible to see the neckline of a blue cardigan, possibly one of many, while across her stomach hung a white muff into which she had plunged her hands.

The Colonel thought she could not be a regular at the pub because Gretchen had not immediately dropped into the Black Country accent which was her preferred mode of speech for those in her circle. The two ladies were at present agreeing that you couldn't trust the weather these days, but it was not long before they switched, as the Colonel had hoped, to the topic of the day. The newcomer ventured the unexceptionable thought that it was all a terrible business. Gretchen's rather more daring opinion was that the police would be lucky if only one of their number was butchered in this way, the sort yow get down here nowadays.

Believing himself to be an honorary participant in any conversation about the murder, Baxter set aside his earlier rejection of Gretchen, gathered up his coat from the back of the chair, clutched what remained of his hot toddy and marched over to the bar.

"Ladies," he said, inclining his bald head to each of them in turn. "I couldn't help overhearing your conversation just now. I have been in discussion with the police this morning. This is going to be a difficult time for all of us. The killer is still on the loose."

"This is the Colonel. He's a lowcal" Gretchen explained to the lady. Then to Baxter, "What do the purloice think?"

"I'm not at liberty to tell you that," said Baxter. Then, to soften the conversation-stopping effect of this pronouncement, added, "I'll tell you why this will turn out to be a much bigger matter than we ... "

He stopped dead. He had been intending to add that in his opinion the case would prove to be about much more than the murder of one young policeman, but he had suddenly caught sight of the hands the woman had withdrawn from her muff. They were truly alarming. For some reason of her own she had allowed her finger nails to grow unpruned and untended. They had now grown long like the talons of a bird of prey. Baxter goggled helplessly at them.

She smiled understandingly, holding one hand up for appraisal. "After the first shock people usually pretend not to notice. If my son had remained, I'm sure he would have told you all about his mother's little conceit."

"That was your son I was speaking to? Young man reading *Sons and Lovers*?"

"The boy who bolted as soon as I came in. Yes, that was Graham. Reading a book. He's at Oxford. They do that sort of thing there."

She offered no further information and Gretchen, in the loud, stretched-out tones of one giving directions to a particularly thick Mongolian tourist said, "This lidy runs the August Moon shop. Boy the Green."

"I re-open at two o' clock." Mrs Moon delicately conveyed a business card to the Colonel, using one of her claws and arousing in Baxter the same kind of admiration he had felt when as a young subaltern dining in the Hong Kong Garrison Mess he had first observed his senior officers' dextrous use of chopsticks. He took it warily, acutely conscious of the fact that in the last few moments he had done something he normally abhorred. He had yielded pole position in a bar room conversation.

And to a woman at that.

* * *

It was one of Kenneth's rules to ask his clients no more about their everyday lives than they volunteered during their scheduled encounters. He kept no records of these, or any other, intimate confessions. He merely noted the times of their appointments by a strictly personal coding arrangement in a Boots Diary. And although his clients all had his private phone number, he did not have any of theirs.

That afternoon's visitor, following upon his exhausting encounter with Julia the previous evening, was making her first visit and had not yet been accorded a code name. She had arrived three minutes before the agreed time and when Kenneth finally answered her repeated ringing of the bell (he disapproved of earliness as much as he disliked the habit of arriving late) he noticed that she seemed unusually distressed about something. She started sobbing as soon as she had got through the door and pulled off her black plastic coat in the hallway. When shown up to the bedroom she had lost her inhibitions completely, torn off her spectacles, begun to howl despairingly and stamp her feet like a three-year old – giving Kenneth's elderly neighbours the worrying impression that an enemy air raid was in progress.

Hysterical scenes were not infrequent in the world of the theatre but in real life Kenneth could not cope with anyone emoting on this scale. He could only pass her a paper tissue and offer the kind of cheesy line he had sometimes been made to utter in out-of-copyright stage plays, "Darling, whatever's the matter?"

The newcomer said nothing in reply, but after a minute or two seemed to realise that she had effectively conveyed that she was somewhat troubled and began to dab more fitfully at her eyes. She started to prepare for the all clear, dropping the sound level and contenting herself with loosing off an occasional gurgle of indrawn breath. Until finally, happily, there was comparative silence. When that was achieved Kenneth felt that, without risking collateral damage to his carefully laundered dressing gown, it was safe to put his arms around her. "There, there," he said softly and, unable to improvise a better line, added, "Poor you. Poor, poor you."

When she had composed herself, he unwound his arms and looked down at her with what he hoped was a compassionate expression. "Do you still want ...?" he asked, indicating what he meant with a sideways inclination of his carefully tonsured head towards the bed, accompanied with a look which he hoped hinted at near uncontrollable lust coupled with intense compassion. Behind her back he glanced at his wrist watch - like Gary Essendine in *Present Laughter*, a part he hoped one day to play - making a mental note of the time (and incidentally noting his pulse rate was normal).

"Yes, yes, I do!" she gasped throatily. Usually, at this juncture, Kenneth would give his client a long smouldering glance and put on a Miles Davies record, but this lady had no time for such fripperies. She began clumsily to undress, strewing her clothing carelessly about the floor, while Kenneth tried to bring some decorum to the scene with vain attempts to fold the discarded clouts into neat piles. Their frantic collisions and entanglements reminded him of an old Fred Karno sketch, *Their Wedding Night*, which he had seen on You tube. He smiled to himself at the memory and then, in case his client should misinterpret the cause of his mirth, quickly divested himself of his dressing gown, reached for her naked body and drew her heavily down on top of him. Her collapsed bulk left Kenneth gasping for breath, while she urgently attempted to impale herself on him.

At first this just proved difficult.

Then impossible.

For all his adult life and throughout his years with Helen, Kenneth had never failed at the appropriate time to provide, as it were, the right tool for the job. Yet now, as his client desperately ground her fleshy haunches against him, his usually proud member was if anything shrinking further into abject retreat.

He was getting ready to mouth his regrets when she fell sobbing on to him, offering instead her own tearful apologies. "It's my fault. You can't do it. How could you bear even to look at me? I know I've lost my looks. I've lost everything. I knew I shouldn't have rung you. You'll never want to see an old bag like me again. Oh, I'm so miserable," and so on.

Unexpectedly exculpated, Kenneth explained in his most compassionate voice that it wasn't her fault at all. He was entirely to blame. He explained caringly that he had *deliberately* avoided getting an erection. (Yet how on earth could you do that? he wondered in passing. Poke it into a packet of frozen peas? Imagine you were shagging the German Chancellor?) Improvising shamelessly, he said he hadn't felt he could take advantage of her, in her distress. Next time, he promised, it would be quite different.

Whereupon and for the first time she looked him in the eyes, smiled damply, sat up on the bed, draped a sheet over her shoulders and told him at some length what had driven her to this desperate act. Her husband, mentioning no names, was a dry old stick whose only enjoyment was going out drinking with his Chamber of Commerce pals. All he thought about these days was his Masonic Lodge. Oh no, she wasn't kept short of money (Kenneth knew that already) and she had a lovely house and all the clothes she wanted. He didn't stop her doing anything. And he wasn't jealous of her. She sometimes wished he would be jealous, more possessive of her at any rate.

"I know exactly what you mean," said Kenneth, who hadn't the faintest idea. She smiled at him again, so that he noticed her mouthful of perfectly white teeth and was momentarily struck with the unfairness of their relative positions in life. She, who made love like a yeti with an inner-ear infection, could nevertheless afford to register as a private patient and have a dental specialist at her beck and call to grind and bleach her molars. Whereas he, an artiste in need of a gleaming set to do either of his jobs properly, had to wait weeks for a dental inspection, which could be with any one of a fluctuating corps of evil-looking foreign dentists. And even then, any promise of treatment would mean being put on a waiting list for about thirty years and you'd still have to re-mortgage your house to pay the bill.

But it was not her fault, any of that. Mustn't get angry with her. He must apply himself to the task in hand. Slowly, as if he were preparing a nervous animal for the auction ring, he began to pat and stroke her generous flanks. Tentatively she responded. At length another part of his body stirred and attracted first his, then her, attention. Quite soon everything had been put right, and she was smiling across at him, with enough strength remaining to ask him how he rated her performance in comparison with all the other women he must have had.

As she happily chattered, Kenneth was considering what her code name should be. 'Sloth' would be right on so many levels, he decided.

* * *

The five-strong murder team – Plover and four trusties - which assembled around the desk in the Inspector's office at two o' clock had for a moment fallen silent.

Harris sat on the Inspector's right, then came WPC Pollard, Inspector Dimmock from D Division and Dickinson from Forensics. They were thumbing through the Coroner's Initial Report - made available only half an hour before – and trying to make sense of what still seemed beyond reason.

Plover called them to order.

"OK. Before we get stuck in, Sergeant Dickinson might have some news." He nodded to him to proceed.

"Somebody called in this morning. An old grey van found parked behind a block of garages in Meads. Didn't belong there. My lads went out, put it in quarantine and brought it in to the lab for a going-over. Let you know as soon as we've got anything." He tapped the smartphone on the desk in front of him.

"Thanks Dickie. So, let's turn to the coroner's report. Photographs aren't very pretty are they?"

Murmurs of agreement. "No they aren't." "Why shoot him then smash his face in?" "Christ, what a mess!" "Did somebody not want him recognised?"

"Some bastard stove the front of his skull in." Harris could always be relied on to state the obvious. "We need to find where they did that," he added, unnecessarily.

"Christ, Harris!"

"Well, you can't mutilate a corpse in your own front room, can you?"

"So where did they kill the poor bugger?"

From around the table came more voices: "Outhouse?" "Garage?" "Somebody's shed?"

"More likely a beach hut," WPC Pollard's familiar Sussex burr. "It's out of season. Less likelihood of being interrupted."

"Good thinking," from Plover, "Search them. Get on to the Council. For the master keys," he added, when Harris looked perplexed.

"But the big question," he went on, "is why Fletcher was targeted. Why did somebody want to kill him?"

"Any form?" asked Dimmock."

"Nothing that I can see."

"Somebody with a grudge against him?"

"They'll target a particular copper for something he's responsible for. He's grassed up their best friend. Had their big brother put away. We've all had threats made against us because of that sort of thing. But as far as I can see, Fletcher had no previous. He hadn't been in the force long enough to cross the paths of any serious villains. He didn't seem to have any bad habits. His file has nothing in it to give us a clue. His colleagues won't say a word against him. He's almost too good to be true, except for …"

"Except for what?" from Dickinson.

"The one thing out of character is that last night he wore his uniform when he was off duty. Why? And I'd give a fortune to know why nobody saw him leave the station? It was early evening. Plenty of people about. We can go through the CCTV. But somebody must have clocked him - walking along Grove Road, waiting for a bus, going through the Arnda – the Beacon – whatever they call it now."

"Unless he was in a car."

"He didn't own a car.".

"Perhaps he was in a pub?"

"He hardly drank. In any case he wouldn't go in to a pub in uniform when he was off duty. Asking for it. But somebody was gunning for him. There's got to be a motive. Got to be." Plover made a brief gesture of surrender and then fell silent, lost in his own turbulent thoughts.

It was at that moment that the phone on the desk trilled. For a brief moment hope flared, but as soon as Dickinson picked up and they saw his expression change, they knew it was no go.

"No luck with that one," Dickinson said cheerfully, "but its early days yet. Don't worry, we'll get him. We'll get him!" He looked up, chin jutting defiantly.

But there was no response from the rest of the room.

***

Fog was descending on the Saffrons when, at twenty-two minutes past six, Julia drove down into Eastbourne and turned into the Town Hall Car Park. Recognising the badge on the People Carrier the attendant, skimpy uniform stretched over a sheepskin coat, gave an officious smirk and indicated that he considered it best if she would agree to park in the bay marked 'Council Guest'. Julia ignored him and drove into it anyway. She had said she would drive herself tonight rather than call out the police car and driver to which she was entitled. She liked to show off her inconspicuous consumption.

As she dismounted other cars were pulling to a stop and from all over the tarmac came the sounds of well-fitted car doors crunching shut, interspersed with gruff, false-sounding, cries of greeting.

The Members of Eastbourne Borough Council were assembling for an Emergency Meeting.

The Leader, Mrs Barbara Muttley, was waiting by the back door to greet Julia, a glistening sable coat draped over her skinny shoulders, whisky fumes faintly discernible on her breath. "Come on in, darling," she said, coughing like a jack hammer and beckoning with a scrawny arm. "This bloody fog!"

Scarcely ten minutes later, when members had taken up their positions in the Council chamber – an extended manoeuvre, as the need to maintain each party's pecking order and the need to meet the requirements of those members sporting hearing aids and other appliances had both to be accommodated - Councillor Muttley stared over at the empty public benches and wheezed reassuringly: "No representatives of the press here tonight. I saw to that." When Julia observed that there seemed to be no witnesses at all to their discussions, the Leader acknowledged the compliment, adding triumphantly, "And we don't publish the Minutes neither!" She gave her familiar Bride of Dracula cackle, "Now darling, how do you want to go on?"

When Julia had told her, the Leader rapped her ball point sharply on the table.

"The Emergency Session shall come to order. The Deputy Area Commissioner is going to give us a summary of the situation arising over the Beachy Head murder. I know that all council members would wish to get involved in this atrocity. So, over to you, Mrs Jackson-Grant."

Julia, who had been updated by Inspector Plover not an hour previously, followed the official line. She gave a carefully edited account of the discovery of the body, and the preliminary findings of the Coroner. She said nothing of her own meeting with Fletcher, nothing about the drugs trade but merely told them that the motives for the murder were not yet established. Nor was it known where the murder and mutilation had taken place. However, to facilitate the necessary searches, the police would be glad of access to all Council properties, including equipment stores, chalets, cellars and backstage areas of the town's theatres. (This was unanimously agreed.) Other search parties were being organised across Newhaven and Eastbourne and other coastal communities, so responsible volunteers would have to be recruited. (Also agreed.) Councillors were asked to pass on immediately to the police any relevant information that came their way. There was no indication that the killer or killers would strike again, but there was nevertheless a need for everyone to take all reasonable precautions when going about their normal business.

She concluded by stressing that it was the police who were responsible for apprehending the killer, and asked Councillors not to give any encouragement to the Eastbourne Vigilantes Group which Brenda Barnaby, the local M.P., had set up in the wake of the Murder. "We can't stop Mrs Barnaby poking her nose into every local cause," she said, amidst laughter, as both the size of the MP's proboscis and her eagerness to poke it into local events were much remarked upon, "but I can assure you that however pure her intentions may be, in this case she is likely to do more harm than good."

Told that Mrs Jackson-Grant was willing to take questions, several gloved hands were raised. Julia assured one acne-riddled youth there would be extra security in the public houses and night clubs. To the Chief Executive, a gap-toothed gentleman whose pink mittens gave him the look of an outsize Easter Bunny, she gave an undertaking that additional policing would not mean that extra cost would accrue to the Borough Council. The Leader of the Opposition, who had an unfortunate stammer, asked whether the police proposed to postpone the Park pantomime. She said they didn't. Nor, she assured other questioners, was there any intention of cancelling the heavily-subsidised exhibition of knotted string currently occupying a small room in the Towner Gallery, nor the upcoming Christmas street market.

There were no more questions. She was fulsomely thanked. Those few Councillors who had chosen to take off their overcoats now thankfully put them back on, while arranging to have just one, or possibly just a couple, at the *Dewdrop* because they didn't want to be back late. By these means, in not much more than an hour and a half the Eastbourne Borough Council had, at least to its own satisfaction, dealt with the emergency.

Meanwhile the fog had thickened. Julia's journey home was slow but, at least in its early stages, uneventful. It was when she turned on to the unadopted side roads leading to her house, where there were no street lights and where the fog wrapped itself more densely around her, that she felt a first shiver of apprehension.

She was now in a strange subterranean world of shapes and shadows. As she inched forward, ghostly fronds from the ornamental trees reached down to touch the car windows, while the red reflector lights on gateposts shone balefully out at her like the bloodshot eyes of crouching daemons.

She grasped the steering wheel more tightly, searching for familiar forms in the enveloping gloom. Though her vehicle was barely crawling, she almost hit the front end of another car parked without lights on the edge of the narrow road. Cursing, she wrenched the wheel to the left and edged the Carrier forward, praying for some familiar sign.

And look! There it was - her own entrance! White-painted driveway gates safely shut, though with the garden gate at the side slightly ajar.

Why was that?

She pressed the keypad to open the main gates, eased through, braked a few yards down the drive, got out and went back to shut the garden gate. Then she stood for a moment by her idling car.

Was everything in order? Usually, when she returned home on a Winter's evening, the bell-shaped light over the back door was turned on in welcome, and a chink of light would be visible shining through the lounge curtains. But tonight she could see only a silent wall of grey.

Julia prided herself on her unflappability. She turned off the engine, switched the headlights off, took her pistol from the glove compartment and closed the car door.

To be met by a grey, breathless silence.

She took a few cautious steps up the drive, but still could discern no light above the back door. Was the light on in the lounge? She stepped off the gravel and on to the roughly-trodden path between the rambling roses. Maybe, if she got close to the window, she'd be able to see the lounge light?

Then she froze.

Something else was in the garden.

Advancing upon her with thudding steps. And getting closer.

Then, with a guttural yelp, it launched itself upon her, clawing, touching and pulling at her legs and arms. She could hear its desperate panting, smell its rank breath, sense its wish to overpower and possess her. Until, just as quickly, the fiend dissolved and took concrete form.

Ben's dog.

Though her heart was still pounding, she bent down on her haunches to make a fuss of him. "Snuff," she cried, "It's you! Are you keeping guard? Good boy!"

Yet even as she spoke she knew that the dog running loose in the garden could be a portent of something evil waiting in the darkness. What had happened to Ben? She straightened up, turned and began to take cautious steps over the icy lawn towards where she judged the French windows to be. The dog padded silently after her. Once arrived there she leaned forward and pressed her face against the securely-locked windowpane. The curtains were open and the lounge was in darkness.

Murmuring to the dog to follow she began to grope her way along the wall, turning the corner before moving on to the concrete ramp and edging up to the back door. As carefully as she could she inserted her key and gingerly began to ease it open. Almost immediately Snuff, impatient to be restored to his familiar environs, had pushed past her and lolloped off down the corridor.

She was about to call him back when she heard somebody greeting the dog, and the sound of its scuffling paws. Surely that was Ben's voice, stentorian and low. "Are you there, love?" she cried, but there was nothing in reply. She called again, "Are you there?"

Still silence. She stood stock still for a moment, listening. A patter of paws and the dog came back down the passage and looked impassively up at her.

She must act as if all was as normal. She clicked her fingers to the dog and set off down the unlit corridor, walking as softly as she could. There was no other sound. She saw the door to the darkened lounge was open, but the door to Ben's study was tightly shut.

Beneath the study door there was a strip of light.

Julia pushed the door open, saw what was within and screamed, "Ben!".

He did not – could not - reply. Sprawled disjointedly before her was her husband, arms tied with rope to his wheelchair, gagged and blindfolded with dirty white towelling. Snuff went up to him and tried, unavailingly, to scramble up on to his master's lap. But the dog's clumsy efforts resulted in some discernible movement in the lower limbs.

Ben was alive.

* * *

It took nearly an hour for Plover and his team to assemble and nose out through the fog to the

Jackson-Grants' house. Finding the drive still blocked by Julia's Carrier, they had parked out on the road, leaving their warning lights flashing.

They found Julia in dominant form and as usual determined to take charge of the investigation. She told them that when she had freed Ben she had phoned Plod and left a message for her Solicitor who had turned his phone off. As soon as she had made sure Ben was all right and had got him a hot drink she'd made a recce of the ground floor, discovering that the French windows in the lounge had recently been opened from the inside - presumably by the intruder when he was leaving the building. She had then, she informed them, undertaken a quick search of the rooms upstairs which showed nothing important had been disturbed and nothing of value taken. Of course, she added, this incident was linked to the murder of P.C. Fletcher. Had to be. Presumably meant as a warning, didn't Plover agree?

"You may be right, ma'am," said Plover, impassively.

"I can't think of any other explanation. Can you?"

"One thing at a time, ma'am."

He shifted his gaze to Ben, "When did you first realise that something was wrong?"

"I didn't realise anything was wrong," replied Ben, snappily. "I was asleep, wasn't I?"

"In your study?"

"That's where I woke up, yes. The last thing I remember before that I was in here, just after six, giving Snuff his evening meal. Julia had gone off to meet the Eastbourne Borough Council."

He gave the dog a comradely pat, as if to corroborate his story. Five of them were sitting around the big kitchen table, Ben by the stove, Harris nearest the door so the boys could reach him if they found anything interesting. WPC Pollard, supposedly there to look after Julia, sitting slightly apart from the others, ill at ease in the company of so many of her elders and betters. "Like a spare prick at a wedding," she informed her fellow constables the following day.

"I must have dropped off," Ben went on, "next thing I knew I was in the study, tied up in the chair. Where Julia found me."

"You dropped off to sleep Ben? Really? That doesn't sound like you. Was your dog with you?"

"No, not after I'd fed him. He usually goes to his basket in my study. But this time Julia found Snuff in the garden. She found him and brought him back in. Just before she came for me."

"And you really don't have any idea how the intruder got in?"

Testily, "No Plod, I don't." At the mention of the forbidden nickname the faintest of smiles crossed Harris's homely features. "In case you hadn't noticed, I am no longer in the force. It's your job to tell me."

Hoping Mrs Jackson-Grant didn't mistake banter between old colleagues for something more serious, Harris sought to redirect the conversation. "At least we know how he got out, don't we ma'am? Through the French windows in the lounge."

"Well, he certainly didn't get in that way," responded Julia. "I can vouch for the fact that when I came home, the French windows were shut tight."

"Why are we assuming it was one man?" asked Plover. "Why not two?"

"Why we assumin' it were a man anyway?" Pollard's accent made her sound like a maid in a TV costume play. "Why couldn't it have been a woman?" She then looked at Plover, wondering whether it had been all right for her to speak.

He didn't look back at her but turned instead to Jackson-Grant. "Well, Ben?"

"I've already said I didn't hear him. Or them. Or her." WPC Pollard looked sheepish. "Or it," he added.

Harris attempted to lighten the mood. "A woman could easily have pushed Ben's wheelchair from the kitchen to the study."

"The intruder was most certainly *not* a woman," snapped Julia. "It was a man. I heard him speak to Snuff."

Further exchanges were checked by the shy entrance of a uniformed officer, who nodded to beg the company's pardon before bending down to whisper something to Sergeant Harris.

"Oh, come on, spit it out," said Plover. "Let's all hear it. Found anything? Prints?"

"No sir. They used gloves."

"Nothing on Inspector Grant's wheelchair?"

"No, sir. Except for Mr and Mrs Jackson-Grants'."

"What about the French windows?"

"None, sir. The same. Just Mr and Mrs Jackson-Grants'."

"Do you know how the intruder got in?"

"The constable looked uncomfortable. "Through the back door, sir." Sensing their disbelief, he jabbered nervously on, "We've looked at every window, every single one, upstairs and down. Looked in the old coal chute, at the conservatory doors, looked at fanlights. No sign of a forced entry anywhere. And there wasn't a window left open by accident, sir. Front door still bolted on the inside. I think whoever was in here tonight, sir, let themselves in through the back door."

And before he could consider the implications, he added the explosive rider, "Or they was let in by somebody."

THREE

The next two scenes in the drama were revealed – in all their dingy horror - on the same day in December. By then search parties had combed through rows of beach huts, council stores, unused garages and through all manner of sheds and outhouses in the area but had found nothing. There had been public appeals for householders to look over their own property and to report anything unusual but that too had drawn a blank. Nor had they any better luck with finding the vehicle they thought had transported Fletcher's body to the lay-by on Beachy Head. The mood among those assigned to the case had started to dip. Even the normally phlegmatic Harris began to think they might never find the means whereby P.C. Fletcher had been done to death.

Then came the first sensation. A Mr Derek Bowskill, who owned a small newsagent's business facing Polegate Station, was looking to rent premises in Eastbourne with a view to opening a second outlet. The shop he had his eye on was empty, and had been so for some time, one of many in and around Terminus Road that had been put out of business by the unfortunately-named 'Beacon', the extended shopping mall that had been intended to enlarge, rather than curtail, retail trade in the town.

Bowskill liked the fact that the shop had a deep interior, with plenty of storage room. It also had generous window space and good potential for passing trade. But, as he ran his Polegate business single-handed, he could only spare time to inspect the premises on a Sunday afternoon. The shop had been on the market for some time. All of the big house agents in the town had tried at various times to offload it but had more or less given up the struggle to sell, particularly on a Sunday and at that time of year. Eventually one of the area's lesser-known agents, Dick Rodham of Newhaven, had agreed to show him around.

The two men were now standing on the litter-strewn pavement looking at the depressing clutch of empty shops ranged before them. "Don't take too much notice of what you see here at present," Rodham advised. "This area is on the up. Town Centre Regeneration," he added confidentially, as if he and his mates in the Chamber of Commerce had inside knowledge of Saudi Princes eager to invest in the renovation of old-fashioned South Coast resorts.

But whatever hopes Eastbourne Borough Council may have harboured for their longer-term investment and development, at present the shops in the area bore all the signs of advanced urban decay. Some of their windows were boarded up; others, such as the premises they were inspecting, were whitewashed over. Lurid posters had then been crudely pasted on to each available space. Some of them were for one-night stands at the local theatres and of recent origin; others, such as a colourful invitation to visit the Bulgarian State Circus in Princes Park, were many months out of date.

The pavement beneath their feet was encrusted with what looked like the droppings of long-extinct animals. The shop doorways by contrast bore signs of more recent habitation. In the case of the shop the two men were entering, this was reinforced by the pungent smell of fresh urine emanating from a pile of sodden rags piled in the doorway. "You'd soon be rid of all that," smiled Rodham, without conviction.

It was another and more ominous smell that assailed them as they stepped into the dark recesses of the shop. A stale but somehow familiar aroma, like a stagnant ditch. "God in Heaven!" cried Bowskill, putting a handkerchief to his nose, "What's died?" "Stand still," said Rodham, "I'll put the light on."

He groped unsteadily through the darkness, looking for the hanging switch that turned on the single working bulb, knocking over what sounded like an empty petrol can, catching his breath as he felt his shoe skidding on some jelly-like substance on the concrete floor.

He found the switch and turned it on.

In the dim light afforded by the gently swinging bulb, they saw the detritus of a human abattoir.

Bloodstains had splashed on to the rear wall. Scattered around the floor were pieces of charred clothing together with petrol cans and two heavy tyre levers. Close by, and more terrible yet, was a crimson pile of what looked like offal. That was what Rodham had trodden in.

Permeating everything, the abominable stench of rotting flesh.

Rodham said "Christ!" then weakly to Bowskill, "I'm terribly sorry. I'd no idea. I'll ring the police."

"God in heaven," muttered Bowskill again.

The swinging bulb threw grotesque shadows on to the bloodstained wall, creating a pulsating pattern of red and black corpuscles, like grubs devouring a beating heart.

When Rodham got through to the Police he could only croak two words: "Come. Quickly."

* * *

As an ashen-faced Dick Rodham was phoning the police, the stage at the nearby Devonshire Park Theatre was full of ruddy-cheeked villagers dancing and singing about how hap-hap-happy they were. And by the time Plover and his team had arrived and were taking in the bloody contents of the disused shop, on the Park stage the happy villagers had scattered at the first rumbustious appearance of the Dame. Meanwhile in the wings, two persons of restricted growth, wearing only G strings, had climbed into the rubbery skin of a comedy cow and were awaiting the Dame's summons on stage. It was the first scene of the annual Christmas pantomime.

Time was when all pantos opened on Boxing Day and the starry ones in the big cities would run through to May or even June. In those days they featured well-known singers and comedians, stars from the variety theatre who were used to working live audiences, and they included specialities – Currie's Waterfalls, Kirby's Flying Ballet, the Dagenham Girl Pipers – which were genuinely spectacular. Nowadays the named artistes were usually youngsters whose acting experience was limited to televised reality shows, the special effects were bits of tired electronic gadgetry and the runs very much shorter. In Eastbourne for instance, the annual pantomime opened half way through Advent and closed soon after the kids went back to school.

None of which was of any immediate interest to Kenneth, who found himself uncomfortably jammed into one of the Devonshire Park's narrow dress circle seats at a Sunday matinee of *Jack and The Beanstalk*. To his left was Soozie, who had agreed to attend this spectacle on condition she could bring her two diminutive nieces, Franny and Soggy, who were at this moment attempting to follow the instructions of Jack, the principal boy. The role of Jack, following a tradition which Kenneth considered to be well past its sell-by date, was taken by a girl - in this case a pasty, vacant-looking girl, a girl whose only claim on public attention was that she had recently reached the finals of a television show called, in defiance of the available evidence, *Britain's Got Talent*.

Having paid brief homage to the plot by selling the comedy cow for a handful of beans, Jack was for no particular reason whiling away the time during his journey home by performing what might in happier circumstances be called an audience-participation song - had the audience been participating. To Kenneth, a purist, it all seemed like the antithesis of a real theatrical experience. Perhaps it was the non-stop chattering of the audience, the clattering of the stage hands assembling the next scene or the obvious inability of Jack to convey anything of significance to anybody more than four feet away from him or her. Whatever the reason, communication between performer and audience had for the moment broken down. There was no sense of urgency on stage. Jack seemed as indifferent to the audience's lack of reaction as they were to his/her instructions. Far from trying to speed up the action, Jack was giving every indication that he/she was perfectly happy to go on like this until midnight.

Meanwhile, up in the dress circle, noticing that Soozie had for the moment withdrawn her attention from the action, Kenneth mimed a vomiting attack and looked questioningly at the exit. Soozie smiled sympathetically but inclined her head to Franny and Soggy, indicating that so long as her young kinsfolk retained some interest in Jack's turgid adventures, t'were kindest to sit it out. Kenneth nodded and looked resigned to his fate.

In any case the chance of making an orderly exit rapidly disappeared as Jack made a sudden inexplicable decision to stop whatever he/she was doing and clumped off towards the wings, accompanied by an equally inexplicable cheer from the audience. The orchestra then made a scraping noise and the next scene ('In the Dame's Garden') was revealed - a painted cottage set within a painted shrubbery, all looking out on a bulky mechanism stage centre which had been inexpertly disguised as an ivy-covered tree stump. No doubt, this was the container from which the beanstalk would magically grow.

But before that could happen, they all had to endure another appearance by the man billed as 'Eastbourne's favourite Dame'. (So, had they held a referendum about this? What was the opposition? And why had he, Kenneth, not been allowed a vote?) Even now, as he pondered these matters, the people's favourite was poncing and shrieking his flabby way downstage. When he had arrived at his destination and uttered his depraved bleat of "Hello Kiddies!", little Franny shrank back into her seat and little Soggy bared her teeth and put her hand over her eyes. Kenneth, who at Central had learned the practices of good children's theatre, copied her gesture, moaning softly to himself.

Following which there was a bit more plot - Jack and his mother arguing over the selling the cow – after which the Dame felt impelled to perform a comedy strip tease routine before entering her cottage. The orchestra then began to strum that well-known sequence of chords – dum, dum, dum, da, dum - da, da, da, da - which signals to pantomime audiences everywhere that a magical event is imminent. The lights narrowed down on the beanstalk's base. Jack, who had remained oblivious both to the Dame's dubious sexuality and to her overall lack of taste, moved over to the tree stump, said something and threw an invisible bean in its general direction. Upon which, the sound from the orchestra became much louder (to drown out the noise of the tree stump's machinery, Kenneth presumed). Additionally, over the loudspeakers, came an unearthly wailing which added to the general din.

Now, amid mounting tension, a single green leaf was seen pushing skywards from the middle of the stump.

Franny and Soggy were leaning forward excitedly in their seats. And so was Kenneth, seemingly caught up in the magic of the moment, as lighting, music and property department for once seemed to be working in harmony.

The ascending fronds waved mysteriously as the beanstalk coiled upwards. The aperture in the tree stump grew wider, the stems became stronger and thicker, the leaves broader and greener ...

But what in God's name was this?

A blood-splattered figure in a white dress was rising jerkily from the tree stump, tendrils knotted around it like the tangled strings of a marionette, shiny bald head bobbing on its broken neck.

A moment's silence then, staring transfixed at the lurid apparition dangling before them, the audience began to scream, at first in fits and starts and then united in one piercing, inhuman shriek.

The stage crew blundered confusedly into action. The beanstalk was checked in its ascent and the corpse lazily swung on its cords, its half-severed throat grinning hideously. The screaming grew to a crescendo. Then the body was gradually masked from the audience by the descending safety curtain. The theatre orchestra, although instructed to play on regardless in any crisis, had disappeared. However, the keening from the loudspeakers continued apace. Out in the auditorium pandemonium reigned. Some of the front-of-house staff were attempting to calm hysterical children. Everyone else seemed to be standing in their seats, yelling or screaming hoarsely.

Colonel Baxter, in life a stickler for cleanliness and good order, would have hated such confusion to attend his death. But he was now beyond such earthly considerations.

* * *

Plover and his police team drove over to the theatre the minute they were called, leaving Dickinson and his colleagues from Forensics poring over the bloody detritus in the shop premises.

Plover rapidly took in the bizarre scene on stage where the cotton-frocked corpse still hung raggedly from the property beanstalk. A smell of bodily effluent. The stage crew stood dazedly about, looking at everything but that hanging, broken body. The performers meanwhile had bolted for the safety of their dressing rooms.

Plover assumed centre stage, deploying his team.

Sergeant Harris, sent to minister to front of house, proved to be an influence for calm. Standing on the apron and using his gentlest voice, he first informed the audience that they had had a bad shock and should sit down for a few minutes during which cold drinks would be available free of charge. Then he told them that management had agreed they could either have their money back, or tickets for later in the run. Although the management had made no such promise, this undoubtedly lightened the mood. Harris then slipped in the third and less palatable announcement that the constables now stationed at the exits would need to know everyone's name and address before they could be permitted to leave. To the mutinous buzz that followed the last announcement he responded by saying, "We shall have to take statements about what you saw. That is very important. We are asking you to work with us as key witnesses."

Behind the safety curtain Plover was less diplomatic. He gathered together the lighting staff, skulking orchestral players, dressers, chaperones, stage manager and crew (whom he forbade from going near the beanstalk mechanism), asked for the stage lights to be extinguished and for working lights to be switched on. Although he was an interloper in their tight little world, the theatre folk instinctively obeyed him, recognising in the DI a genuine authority figure.

Plover took a microphone from the stage manager:

"I have rushed here this afternoon from another crime scene. Plainly something terrible is occurring in this town. I am sorry you have to be a part of it, but you are now involved, I'm afraid. What my colleagues have to do now will take them some time. We shall have to examine all the stage mechanisms, and to interview each of you. There will of course be no performance tonight. Or tomorrow, I expect. This afternoon, as we pursue our inquiries, nobody will be allowed to leave the theatre without my express permission. And remember that you'll help us most by remaining calm and answering our questions as fully and completely as you are able."

So saying, Plover motioned to his men to cover the doors and walked up the steeply-raked stage to the dressing room entrance reflecting, as he passed the rubber skin of the cow and a rack of the Dame's clothing, that producers of pantomime do rather make it difficult for themselves.

By the mechanical beanstalk, two men from Forensics were already pulling on their white suits and moving over to dismantle it. A police photographer clicked relentlessly.

Dimmock beckoned to the stage manager to help him winch down the body.

So the inquiry into Colonel Baxter's death and bodily mutilation was begun. By six thirty, when the corpse was wheeled off the stage to begin its journey to the Mortuary, it had amongst much else been established – thanks to the dead man's habit of having complete name tags stitched on to every piece of his apparel - that these were the mortal remains of Colonel Richard Broadribb Baxter, of Iris Cottage, Alfriston, East Sussex. The cotton dress, which bore the name tag of a well-known firm of theatrical costumiers, had plainly been picked up backstage and arranged on the body after death.

Dimmock wanted to know how and when the murderer could have got the body into the property tree stump.

Where was the tree stump kept? The stage manager explained that at each performance, as soon as the garden scene finished, the stump was parked in the (actors' left) wings with the various fronds of the beanstalk coiled up inside it, as per the hirer's instructions. An hour before each performance its mechanism was put on charge. So, from the time the cast and crew started arriving at the theatre until the last person left the building, it was always in plain sight of cast or crew.

However, under cover of the night hours anyone could, in theory, have stowed a body within the stump's entrails. They would however have been taking a risk as during the night a burglar alarm, linked to the police station, automatically switched itself on. This device was highly sensitive to movement. Even rats had been known to set it off, summoning policemen to flash their torches into all the recesses on stage and in the auditorium, looking for human intruders. But the burglar alarm had not been activated since October, even by rats.

For his part, as soon as he had descended the dressing room stairs and taken in the high emotion on display Plover realised that rational discourse was impossible. He gave up any thought of forbidding the use of mobile phones as several of the performers were already whimpering into them. The Dame, having discarded his wig and comedy bosom, was consoling a sobbing giant. The actors of restricted growth, who earlier had given life to the comedy cow, were sitting side by side in their dressing room, turning the pages of a photograph album.

"We loved Richard Baxter," said one, as Plover walked by.

"More than life itself," added the other.

Plover abruptly turned back. "Why do you say that?" he demanded.

"Because he's dead and gone sweetie. That's his body hanging there."

"Rest his soul."

"How do you know this? Did you know Colonel Baxter?"

A wheezy chuckle. "Everybody knew Dickie Baxter, darling."

The Giant, who had detached himself from the Dame's embrace and taken up a position behind Plover's left shoulder, said, "Benji's right. We all knew him."

"Very well," said Plover evenly, "Then I'll speak to you all about him." And, as he passed back down the short corridor, he saw Jack wearing a cotton dress and sitting apart from the rest of the troupe, filing her nails. He asked her, "Did you know Colonel Baxter?" She was silent for a moment, then gave a decisive shake of the head. "I never met him," she said.

As he regained the stage Dimmock beckoned him over.

"We think we've identified the body. It was …"

"Colonel Baxter!" cried Plover, "I know. I know. *Everybody* knew Colonel Baxter, ducky."

* * *

Lured by the insidious summons of social media, crowds gathered in silence around the theatre. Individuals of varied hues and shapes knocked at the stage door, all claiming their inquiries were in the public interest. Most of them – particularly the stringers for the national press – were refused admittance. A few were looked on with more favour.

One such was the Eastbourne Theatres Maestro, Mandrake, a Russian Émigré who claimed to have learned his trade at the Bolshoi. He said he voss spitting tacth because people had been given their money back without hith permission. The pantomime wath one of his main thources of income!

He was soothed by Harris, who first frightened him a little, then flattered him, then solicited his assistance. Mandrake proved highly susceptible to all three approaches. By the time his conversation with the Sergeant was over he had agreed to supply the police with full information about all the theatre routines. He began by explaining who, apart from himself, had pass keys to the theatre – the list included the house manager, catering manager, various council employees, the police and the fire service. He also agreed that Tuesday's, and indeed Wednesday's, performance could if necessary be cancelled.

Dickinson was the second to gain admittance. He came to report that his team had for the moment finished examining the grisly contents of the shop. They had taken a number of DNA swabs and dozens of prints but they were not optimistic that they would reveal anything new, as the assailants had been careful to leave nothing of themselves behind. He had sent samples from the piles of offal to the lab., although it was obvious what it was and from whom it had been torn. One other point of interest was that the charred jacket found on the premises still had its name tag in it and belonged to Colonel Richard Broadribb Baxter, of Iris Cottage, Alfriston. "Brilliant! Long live forensics!" cried Dimmock, sarcastically.

The cast had left the dressing rooms and slunk off to their digs when the third visitor arrived. Plover had been half-expecting her. Though even when half-expected Brenda Barnaby M.P. was not a pretty sight - particularly when, as now, the veteran politico was wearing her 'deeply concerned' look, as if she had television cameras constantly trained upon her. Mrs Barnaby's long grey hair was swept back, away from her forbiddingly-pointed nose – a frequent butt of the political cartoonists – as if some impish agent of natural selection had tried to streamline her head. She clasped the inspector close to where her bosom might have been, stared at Plover's forehead with a show of comradely sympathy and began speaking in stentorian tones which, had there been no impediment to their transmission, would surely have carried all over her Eastbourne Constituency,

"My friends, I am here to offer my deepest sympathy, and to assure you that the Eastbourne Vigilantes group will tender your inquiries the fullest cooperation.

We must work together to rid our beautiful town of the stain of these terrible events."

Plover had the sense of a photograph being taken. Then Barnaby released him and said in quite a normal voice, "Tell me what I can do."

"Let's talk," Plover said and, motioning Harris to accompany them, led the way downstairs to the dressing rooms. They arranged themselves uncomfortably in the Dame's lair, bare now save for an oversized pair of rubber breasts hanging from a peg, and a few silver-framed photographs of bare-chested young men by his make-up box. "First of all," said Plover, "I want to warn you about something."

Harris watched Mrs Barnaby raise her chin and snap into an exaggerated 'I'm listening' mode. He decided anew that he disliked all politicians.

"Whoever is responsible for these atrocities is almost certainly known to us," Plover began. "He or she is not an outsider. They have their ear to the ground. They seem to know the inside workings of the Council, and the Police Force - and of the theatre, come to that. So, I want you first to show me a list of the members of your Eastbourne Vigilantes Group, because," Plover added, seeing the MP start to bridle, "the killer will almost certainly have already taken the precaution of joining that body."

"Do you really think so? That's terrible! In that case of course you can see the list."

"And I should be grateful if you would also let me know in advance of any independent actions you or your group propose to take. It's for your own safety as much as anything."

Mrs Barnaby, who valued her own safety highly, said "Of course" again.

"What I am going to tell you now," Plover went on, "is in the strictest confidence. I must have your word that you will not divulge any of it." He leant forward in conspiratorial fashion. Barnaby did likewise, and Plover began to speak. He gave a brief summary of the afternoon's events and told Barnaby in sombre tones what was already common speculation, namely that something else – some criminal conspiracy - lay behind these horrendous events and that when they discovered its nature, they would uncover the criminal. They were hopeful of making an early arrest, he added.

Mrs Barnaby promised that wild horses would not drag this information from her.

At that moment Harris suddenly started. His movement was not in admiration for the way Plod had so easily spiked Mrs Barnaby's guns, nor because of the discomfort caused by his bulk being shoehorned into a plastic stacking chair but because he, Harris, had suddenly remembered what had struck him as odd when he'd visited Baxter's Cottage the day after Fletcher's murder.

FOUR

"It was seeing the Dame's photos in that dressing room, in gilt frames" said Harris, "when I remembered what had struck me when I came here the morning after Fletcher's murder."

There were three of them in the dining room of Baxter's cottage. By the heavy sideboard Harris was talking quietly to Plover, while Mrs Tomkins, Baxter's housekeeper, who had been summoned to show which keys opened which locks and what was stowed where, was sitting mutely at the head of the polished table, pretending not to listen. From upstairs came the sound of drawers being opened and emptied, as the police began their methodical search of the Colonel's possessions.

"You didn't ask him the reason for it?"

"Didn't strike me as important, sir. I'd come here to ask him whether Ben Jackson-Grant was one of his birdwatchers. Didn't occur to me Baxter might be a suspect. Or a victim, come to that."

"But you're sure the photograph was standing here, in its frame? Like this?" Plover indicated PC Fletcher's smiling image on top of the sideboard.

"Certain."

"This is the official mug shot. The one they put out to the television."

"I know that, sir. That's why I thought it was odd. Why did Baxter have that portrait of Fletcher, all framed up, on his sideboard?"

Plover gestured towards the other display frames. "Those look like family photos to me. Perhaps Fletcher was a relative?"

"Perhaps."

"Or one of the birdwatching group."

"Could be."

A young policeman came in, bearing two official-looking ledgers. "Were them what you was looking for, sir?"

"Yes," said Harris. Plover took both books, opened one, shut it and opened the other. "Membership lists," he murmured, running his finger down a page. "I wonder how long Colonel Baxter had acted as Membership Secretary?"

"Four years," cried Mrs Tomkins suddenly. "That old man come here and ask him to do it."

"What old man?"

"Can't remember his name. Colonel Baxter might have told me but I can't remember. He had a big car, a Jaguar."

"Did he come often to see the Colonel?" asked Harris, "Would you recognise his face?"

"Wait a minute," said Plover, looking up from the ledger. "Was his name Mollison? Clifford Mollison?"

"That's right! Mollison!" She nodded with satisfaction, as if she had finally succeeded in getting these dim coppers to accept some awkward but incontestable truth.

"I know Mollison," Plover said. "Solicitor on The Avenue. It appears from this he was the last membership secretary before Baxter." He turned back to Mrs Tomkins and said in a conversational tone, "I wonder, Mrs Tomkins, why it is you're so sure it's been four years since the Colonel took over?"

"They had a row. After the Colonel takes over, committee meets here every month. They has to have refreshments."

"Of course. You make their refreshments. How many were on the committee?"

"Five. Seven. You couldn't never be sure."

"The Colonel, being a tidy-minded sort of man, will have kept a record of those meetings. A Minute Book.

You wouldn't by any chance know where it is, would you?"

A look of mild alarm. "Could be anywhere. He squirrelled things away, the Colonel. I didn't never go in some of his cupboards. Could be upstairs in one of his private stores. What he said he had his things in."

"Do you have keys to them?"

"I got the keys, course I have, but I never looked in them stores," cried Mrs Tomkins, with a righteous indignation which suggested to the police that she certainly had - and moreover that she had discovered something disreputable in them.

Their instincts were right on both counts. "Bloody 'ell," said the normally imperturbable Harris, when the small bedside cupboards had been opened and they were looking at the contents. Tipped out on to Baxter's bed were a pile of cheap sex toys – dildos, fur-lined handcuffs, spiked collars, truncheons – together with poorly-made 'uniforms' including what looked like a delinquent teenager's idea of a Nazi General's outfit. There was also a pile of glossy magazines celebrating the male physique, which nobody seemed to want to open. "Hell's bells," said Dickinson, softly. "Hell's balls, more like," somebody said, "I thought he looked at birds." "The fan-tailed Nancy," suggested another wit.

"Stow it" said the Inspector, amiably enough. And his colleagues, remembering that old Plod was gay, for a moment looked apologetic. But Plover brushed the awkwardness aside:

"Dickie, I want any prints you can get from any of this stuff. Quick as you can."

* * *

Until the accident Ben and Julia had enjoyed a full and rewarding sex life. Ben formerly had something of a reputation as a philanderer, albeit a discreet one, but after their unexpected marriage had found fulfilment in his wife, who so powerfully combined elegance with earthy sensuality. So far as Julia was concerned, after her unsatisfactory years with Harry Jackson, Ben's prowess in bed was a revelation. He also took his part in the management of their household, which her first husband had never done. Further and wonderfully, he found no difficulty in accepting the fact that she was senior to him in the hierarchy of police management. In public, they were admired as a handsome and successful couple. In private they indulged their passion for good food, fine wine and athletic sex.

That is, until the accident.

One August day, at four o' clock in the afternoon, Julia's phone had rung with the first garbled intimation of the head-on crash. She had rushed from the office and driven wildly out to Hailsham. She recalled the drama in short vivid scenes. As she approached the roundabout she had seen the lights of the police cars and ambulances winking in the distance like some ghostly fairground. She'd screeched to a stop, run forward and taken in the horrific detail - the Fire Engine by the crumpled BMW and the Suzuki shunted into the ditch with its back wheels jutting over the kerb.

Stumbling forward breathlessly, desperately willing Ben not to be dead.

The firemen grouped around the crushed car, the machinery prising apart the tortured metal sheets, Ben's chalk-white face and the tangle of bloodstained bandages where his legs had been. One burly fireman had stood in her way, caught hold of her elbow, spun her round, trying to prevent her from looking on the carnage. So she faced the other car, upended, its hatch door burst open, with a paramedic on guard at its side. Two shapes, covered by white sheets, sat still and lifeless in the Suzuki's front seats. In its rear a jumbled mass of cloth and paper and what looked like the remains of a picnic hamper.

As Julia stared, she became aware of some movement, something alive inside the Suzuki's half-open hatch door. The cloth inside was moving, seemed almost to be breathing. Then she saw a snout and a pair of liquid eyes and finally the front half of a hairy dachshund, looking down at the unusual angle and preparing to jump. She shouted a warning and the paramedic spun round. But Julia, ever a lady of action, jumped forward and scooped up the trembling dog in her arms.

Carrying the dachshund, she retraced her steps. This time the burly fireman spoke. "They're getting him out," he said matter-of-factly, "He'll live." There was no warmth in his voice and it occurred to Julia that he probably talked like that because he did not know who she was, had her down as a journalist or maybe even a casual rubbernecker. She inclined her head towards the wreck from which Ben's disjointed body was tortuously emerging.

"I'm his wife. You phoned me and asked me to come here. I'm his wife!" she repeated. "His wife!"

"Uh huh." This time the fireman took it in. The glance he gave her now was one of belated acknowledgement but chiefly, and hardest of all to bear, it was a look of profound pity

* * *

After the hardships of hospital visiting and of enduring the cloying sympathy of her friends, Julia seemed delighted when, a mere fourteen weeks after the accident, her husband was discharged from hospital.

Though their lives together were now very different.

The one inescapable difference was that Ben was permanently confined to a wheelchair. For the first few weeks of home life he was attended by a firm of home carers who, it was thought, could see to all his needs. That was the hope. The downside of the arrangement was that persons of varying age, nationality and intelligence entered the house by means of the new key safe at wholly unpredictable times. With the result that after Julia had left for her office, Ben's breakfast might be served at eleven o' clock by an angry Polish gentleman who did not understand English and did not know what Golden Syrup was, to be followed perhaps an hour later by a garrulous Thai girl who believed in Feng Shui and surreptitiously rearranged the lounge furniture as Ben ate his frugal lunch. There was also Julia's oft-voiced suspicion that the carers, finding themselves in an affluent, well-appointed and seemingly unguarded home, were helping themselves rather too liberally to its contents.

Home care was thus tried and found wanting. Julia sacked the caring firm, refusing to pay their cancellation fee and instead arranged for a private nurse to come in twice a day when she was there and to sleep in when she wasn't. Other caring duties she assumed herself. Ben adapted well enough to this domestic regime but missed his police work - amusing himself by poring over the details of current police investigations and thinking how much better he would have handled them. Otherwise his main pleasure lay in looking after the dachshund that Julia had rescued and then adopted and who, with a mordant sense of irony, they had named Snuff.

Yet despite its determined patina of mutual affection their lives were not – and could never be - the same.

This was particularly true of their sex life. The surgeons had miraculously repaired the upper organs in Ben's shattered body, so he could eat and drink as he ever did, and could taste, see, and hear as well as anybody in their mid-forties, but the surgeons could not restore life to his shattered legs nor, alas, to what remained of his reproductive equipment. The penis that Julia had worshipped in their most intimate moments was no longer in working order. For a while they attempted to ignore the problem, hoping their newly-found platonic friendship would alone suffice. Yet such companionship was not enough for Julia, who found that despite her efforts to suppress such longings, she still craved sexual fulfilment. It was her nature. She was through and through a sexual being.

They had sessions in which Ben tried to stimulate her by other means, but they proved less than satisfactory. Achieving a digitally manipulated climax was for Julia even less satisfactory than masturbating herself, and it left Ben more ashamed than ever of his inadequacies. When she lied and said it didn't really matter, that made it worse, for Ben knew how Julia valued full physical commitment in lovemaking. In spite of all that they did not want their comfortable social partnership to be destroyed. But they had to find an answer to the sex problem.

Over the following weeks and months, they continued compulsively to talk about it whenever they were alone together, gradually edging towards the logical solution.

At first it repelled them both but at least it would give Julia a fuller sex life. And it need not lead them to destroy their easy companionship.

They agreed, in a word, that Julia should pay for sex.

She would keep nothing about the arrangement from her husband and tell him everything he wanted to know.

That way, there would be no threat to their friendly marriage.

But there remained one huge difficulty. How on earth could one find a reliable male partner in Lewes or the surrounding area? There were male prostitutes of course, but they ruled themselves out by plainly being on the lookout for gay men and even thinking of what that might involve was repugnant to Julia. Perhaps a more suitable partner might be found in London, but regular visits up to town would surely excite interest. No, her lover had to be local.

It seemed to be an intractable problem until one day, in her capacity as Assistant Area Commissioner, Julia was riffling through a confidential internal document from the Vice Squad detailing the various sex services, legal and illegal, then being advertised in the South East region. Those organisations suspected of using illegal immigrants, mainly in the Brighton and Worthing areax, were flagged up to be visited or raided. Julia had no more than a passing interest in this and ticked each proposed raid without much interest. What genuinely caught her attention however was a copy of a discreet advertisement from a keep-fit magazine in which a well-educated man offered himself as a manly but sophisticated escort for ladies 'of all ages', who 'guaranteed satisfaction' and who gave an Eastbourne telephone number. Eastbourne was not very far from Lewes.

For a few days she held back, worried that she might be putting her professional life and reputation at risk. When she decided to act she asked Ben to make the first contact to suss out whether the advertiser was genuine. Ben duly made the call, but the advertiser refused to speak in any detail until the lady herself phoned him. When Julia did, he gave her an ex-directory number to ring and after they had spoken for several minutes, he invited her to meet him for a morning coffee.

Which led to their first tryst in Kenneth's Old Town maisonette. It was a pure release for Julia, while Kenneth felt a fulfilment he had not enjoyed since his earliest days with Helen. Subsequent meetings were frequent, passionate and thrilling for them both. And Julia kept to her side of the bargain by telling her husband the salient details about these engagements. Ben, though sometimes struggling to accept the new parameters of their relationship, tried hard to be pleased for her.

However, there was one aspect of these transactions which, out of concern for Ben's feelings, Julia did not choose to divulge. It was that Kenneth had fallen in love with her.

And was her devoted slave.

* * *

The unsolved murders remained front page news and the days leading up to Christmas bristled with tension. In the coastal towns people hurried quickly along the pavements, not meeting each other's eyes, eager to return to the safety of their homes. The streets of Eastbourne seemed particularly empty that year, despite the *Herald's* exhortation to keep calm and carry on. The shops in the Beacon resounded to recorded yuletide music, but it echoed down empty aisles. The Devonshire Park pantomime was particularly badly hit, with tickets returned for every performance. And the show itself had to be rewritten, removing all reference to a beanstalk, which rather took away the point.

Rumour had it that some of the town's seafront hotels had shut down for the duration rather than continue to pay staff for waiting on empty rooms. And whereas in previous years crowds had sometimes gathered to watch the light display projected on to the clock tower of the Town Hall, this year people scuttled past, heads down, as if they feared divine retribution if they gave any sign of enjoyment.

It was in that same Town Hall that tonight's Borough Council Reception was to be held. The town's movers and shakers had been informed that the entertainment would still go ahead, 'as a gesture of solidarity with the families and friends of the murder victims'. As proof of the Council's concern, Colonel Baxter's elder sister had been invited (though it was subsequently discovered that she was dead) as had Keith Fletcher's parents, but they could not see the point of making the long and expensive journey from Sheffield to attend what looked to them like a works dance. A few locals had professed to find this exploitation of grief distasteful. Julia for example had indicated that she would not be using her complimentary ticket. Those who had chosen to attend were no doubt reassured to hear that security officers would be 'in attendance'.

Clutching her invitation Gwen Mollison was smiling roguishly at herself in the hall mirror, twisting her abundant auburn hair into a sort of hoodie shape. The effect was less saucy than she hoped, rather of some suspected witch at whom a yokel had just hurled a juicy cowpat.

"Cliff," she called, "We should be going."

There was an apologetic whinny from upstairs and the sound of gushing water. Gwen checked again on the gift-wrapping around the parcel she held which, despite the effort she had put in to disguise its shape, plainly contained a bottle.

The Council Leader had requested the favour of their attendance at six o' clock. It was now twenty to six. She called again, "Hurry, dear. You know what parking's like in town this time of year."

"Coming, coming," Clifford Mollison could now be seen descending the stairway in segments, his calves and ankles first, then, step by step, the rest of his angular frame came into view. He stood facing his wife in the hallway. "You smell nice," he said, then corrected himself, "No, Gwen, you look nice," before destroying the effect entirely, "Those spectacles really suit you." But instead of coldly upbraiding him, as would once have been her wont, she chucked him affectionately under the chin, "Darling you are useless at paying compliments. We shall have to enrol you in charm school, shan't we?" "I suppose we shall," said Clifford warily. Yet her inexplicable good mood continued and lasted for the whole of the car journey into town, even extending to her asking him what he would like on the stereo, and not tearing him off a strip when he asked for Abba.

This benevolence had been in evidence for some days, to Clifford's puzzlement. It did not even disappear after they had pulled up in the 'Councillors' Perks' car park behind the Town Hall and made their way to the back door, which was incongruously draped in black crepe and sprigs of plastic holly. Councillor Barbara Muttley hugged her friend Gwen and offered them both a carefully modulated greeting; "Hello, Gwen my dear. Hello Clifford. This is a sad time. Merry Christmas." They handed over their gift, which was duly added to the formidable cache of malt whisky bottles on the table behind her.

Once they had navigated the franchised-out cloak room 'hang n'pay' system, they entered the hall set aside for the civic revels. It smelled faintly of pine disinfectant and bleach, like an airport lavatory. Hoping that their presence was being noted by their affluent neighbours, the Mollisons took their miniature glasses of mulled wine and mingled with the other celebrants.

"Hello, you two," murmured Plover. Out of uniform he looked uncomfortable. He was wearing a blue blazer and a slim red bow tie, which looked as if it might light up and spin.

"Not working tonight?" Clifford asked pointedly.

"Harris is holding the fort. I'm back on duty later."

Gwen had meanwhile fallen into conversation with a woman with unusually long finger nails. "Do you know Mrs Moon?" she said. "Yes, I do," said Plover, "I know her." "You must all keep your distance," cried Mrs Moon, "Inspector Plover has been interrogating me. I am a murder suspect." "I am Clifford Mollison," said Gwen's husband, frowning in puzzlement at the laughter this provoked.

A grey-haired figure, with an orange top and a blue skirt, was now slicing its way towards them through the crowd. "Christ, it's that awful woman," said Mrs Moon, affecting to wave at somebody the other side of the room and moving quickly off into the throng. "Good evening to you all," said the newcomer. "Brenda Barnaby," she announced, suggesting by her tone that giving her name was a superfluity, as everyone in the room would surely know her. "Good evening Inspector Plover. Good evening Mr Mollison." "Brenda, do you know my wife Gwen?" asked Clifford. "Charmed," said Mrs Barnaby looking past her across the room, "Was that Mrs Moon you were talking to just now? I wanted a word with her, but I keep missing her." "Well, you can have two words with me," said Gwen Mollison playfully, but Mrs Barnaby just frowned and fiddled with her hearing aid, which was her invariable tactic when she wanted to pretend she hadn't heard.

There was a whistling howl from the public address system, and Councillor Muttley was heard to inquire whether this bloody thing was on or not? A moment later, following an ascending series of atmospheric squeals, she came on air to announce that dancing would now begin, and welcomed somebody or other's swinging combo. This was the cue for an extended crash from the platform stage as if somebody had slowly emptied a basket of cracked china on to it. Simultaneously spotlights picked out the culprits - a group of debauched-looking youths, one of them in a vest and trilby hat, another wearing outsize earrings to match his flowered dress, all of them crouched over glittering electronic instruments from which now issued a jangled and strangely unrhythmic stream of sound.

One or two couples took to the floor but the majority shuffled guiltily to the crowded perimeter, murmuring apologies for being 'a bit too old for this sort of thing'. The resultant jam meant that the waiters bearing trays of drinks could not find a way through the crowd and some of the guests, unused to spending more than a few minutes without alcohol, complained that it was always like this when the Council organised something, they didn't know the meaning of good customer relations. And began to make mutinous arrangements to take their custom over the road to *Bibendum*.

Having successfully detached herself from the Mollisons, Mrs Moon was now engaged in smiling conversation with two new men, a pink-faced cleric and a softly-spoken, rather unhappy-looking young man that Mrs Moon had just introduced as her son Graham. Mrs Moon's smile was a little strained as the Oxford-educated priest was asking her son about his supervisors and the youth was stonewalling him. She said something in appeasement and then, seeing Brenda Barnaby's formidable hooter homing in upon her, turned in desperation to Mandrake, the

Eastbourne Theatres Supremo. "Is the pantomime running again?" she asked. "Yeth, it'th running again," replied Mandrake. "But I can't tell you how much money we've lost." "You mean you won't be able to enjoy your holiday in the Cayman Islands this year?" smiled Mrs Moon. "Prethithely!" came the indignant reply.

A few yards away Dick Rodham had attached himself to Mollison and was talking excitedly, waving his arms about a lot. Mrs Moon thought that the picture they presented together suggested a fastidious philosophy don forced by some new 'equality in education' policy to give a tutorial to a half-witted juggler. Though, just to keep the record straight, at that precise moment Rodham was saying to Mollison, with a further expansive wave of his arms, "They're all here tonight - the great and the bad."

There followed another short bout of anguished screaming from the public address system, and Councillor Muttley announced the first song of the evening would be a number from *Evita*. It would be sung by our very own Wanda Miranda, who would then be going on to the Devonshire Park Theatre where she was starring in *Jack and the Giant's Ladder*. Mention of the scene of the recent atrocity did nothing to lighten the general mood and Wanda, whose lowered neckline and split skirt also failed in this respect, took to the stage amidst low expectations. The performance did nothing to raise them. By the time the group had finished their introduction and Wanda's reedy voice could be heard telling Argentinians the fact was she'd never left them, heads were already turning away and conversations resuming.

Rodham took another drink and asked Mollison, "Is Ben Jackson-Grant here tonight?"

"I don't think so," said Mollison, "I haven't seen him anyway. Why?"

"There's something important I have to discuss with him."

"And what is that, pray?"

"I can't tell you, I'm afraid."

"Well, I don't really want to know. I was just making conversation."

"It's about the murders."

"I certainly don't want to hear about it then."

"You'll hear soon enough."

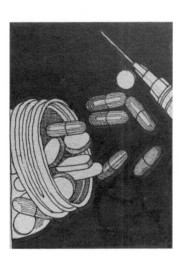

FIVE

On Christmas Eve Ben and Julia held the last of a series of small luncheon parties. They asked on the invitations that the subject of the murders should not be broached at their festive board.

Their guests were the Lewes MP and his husband Brian, Mrs Moon, accompanied by her son Graham (Julia was repaying Mrs Moon's invitation to her Halloween Party) and Dick Rodham, who was a late and hurried addition to the company. The reason for his invitation was that after Rodham had pestered him for several days, Ben had finally agreed to hear what he had to say. The simplest way of effecting this, without interfering with the rest of the Jackson-Grants' busy Christmas schedule, was to invite him to their lunch on the 24th and for Ben to talk to him afterwards. "I think he's some sort of Estate Agent," said Ben, apologetically. "Well, nobody's perfect," said Julia.

His presence nevertheless cast a blight on the gathering. He began by surveying the other guests and saying that if he'd known partners were invited he would of course have brought his wife, who was at a loose end today as she was waiting for him to drive them both to relatives in Essex. He then, having asked for a dry sherry, proceeded to wipe the rim of his glass before drinking, a procedure he went through with every piece of Julia's impeccable cutlery, wiping knives, forks and spoons on his napkin before sullying his mouth by contact with them. Nor was his conversation any more elevated. At one stage the talk turned to the mating habits of various birds and Ben pointed out that penguins were, so far as was known, the only birds which encouraged prostitution. The female of the species would, said Ben, sell her favours for coloured stones. Whereupon Rodham had dug Mrs Moon in the ribs and said he would bet she'd need more than a few pebbles before she came across with a bit of the other and guffawed loudly. There was more in similar vein.

After lunch came a short respite. When the coffee and Mint Thins had done the rounds Graham, egged on by Mrs Moon, agreed to entertain the company with a display of conjuring. Ben, himself an amateur magician, was impressed not only by his tricks but by the professionalism of his patter. Graham's method was first to explain how a trick was done then, as he demonstrated the technique, he would produce an entirely different outcome. For example, he showed his audience how phoney mystics, supposedly possessed of second sight, would allow themselves to be thoroughly blindfolded, yet could still 'see' in front of them. As a demonstration of this 'second sight' he encouraged the local M.P. to bind three napkins over his eyes, then correctly identified various objects pointed to, or held up for scrutiny, not in front of him but behind his back! "Wunderbar!" shouted Dick Rodham amid the general applause.

When it was time for the other guests to leave Rodham had to back his car, which was of course blocking the driveway, out into the road. When he ran back inside Julia coldly indicated that he should join her husband and Snuff in the study while she continued clearing up.

Ben was cocooned in the glow of his desk light. "Now what was it you wanted to tell me?" he asked as Rodham was settling himself.

"The murders. I'm pretty sure I know who the killer is."

"If you've got any information relating to those crimes you should inform the police, not me. The man you want is Peter Plover. He's in charge of the investigation. Nothing to do with me," Ben repeated, though conscious that he had, since the Fletcher murder, scarcely thought of anything else.

"I know that," said Rodham, "but if I'm right, it involves some people in the police force. Including old Plod. What I really need is some tactical advice. I don't want to be disembowelled and strung up on a beanstalk like Baxter."

Ben was silent for a few moments and then looked up. "OK, let's hear it."

"The night of Fletcher's murder. When you were bird-watching on Beachy Head. Me and a few of the gang from the Chamber of Commerce were having drinks. At East Dean."

"So I believe,"

"Well, I noticed then that Cliff Mollison wasn't drinking much. Unlike his normal form."

"So what? Perhaps he's trying to lose weight."

"Cliff? Lose weight? Oh, I see. Pulling my leg. Very good. Anyway, he thought nobody noticed, but during the evening he left the pub. I made a note of the time. Away about an hour."

"I was told his wife picked him up?"

"Yes, she did. But later, at the end. And he was pretending to be drunk – a lot drunker than he was."

"Is that all?"

"No. Mollison knew Colonel Baxter."

"So did I. What of it?"

"Did you know they had a row? Over the Birdwatching Society?"

"Yes, I knew. A while back," Ben was sounding irritated. "I've been a member of that society for three years. I should say Baxter was an easy man to have a row with."

"I also knew that Mollison was away from his office the day Baxter was killed. I checked with his secretary. She doesn't know where he was."

"She never does. And if you're trying to tell me that Mollison is the killer, I'd have to say you need a lot more evidence than that."

"It's not just that the times all fit. I've been watching him. At Chamber of Commerce. And in Lodge. He's acting very strangely. I haven't mentioned it to a soul. But I think that Plover and some of the Masons are shielding Mollison. Well, I can't very well take my suspicions to the police, can I? I know I need more evidence, but what kind of evidence? I want you to advise me."

"I advise you to keep schtum. Listen, one murder inquiry's much like any other. Everyone has a theory, the wilder the better. And then up will pop those dimwits who confess to having done it, just for a bit of publicity. But if you're really going to crack a case like this you'll first have to find a suspect with two very important qualities - motive and opportunity. Get those right and then you can start worrying about details.

Your chap had the opportunity, but so had lots of other people. Much more important, he didn't have a motive. So, I'm telling you son, your theory won't fly."

Nevertheless, when a disappointed Rodham had taken his leave, Grant spent several minutes writing in the blue notebook he kept in a locked drawer of his desk.

* * *

"It's no good trying to talk your way out of it, Ariadne. The police are not the fools you take them for," said Inspector Bull quietly.

"But fings aint allus what they seem, Guv!" This gravel-voiced interjection from a short bald man in a khaki tee shirt with a painted-on five o' clock shadow, "Give 'er a break!"

The cameras tracked gratefully back to the blonde in the revealing white robe, who was draped artlessly over the red divan in the pub's back room. She spoke in an unusually laboured Italian accent, "Ees no good Albert," with a little sob and a heave of her bosom, "Zey 'ev got me. I keeled heem."

The Inspector nodded emphatically, hoping to get into shot, but the cameras stayed resolutely on the blonde's capacious breasts.

Then the big climax. Thrusting her hands out in readiness for the handcuffs, "All right! Eenspector, take me!"

A pregnant pause. Then, "OK, cut!" came a voice from the shadows. "Did you feel ok with that, love?"

"Better, darling," said the man in the tee shirt, "but I do think the punters should see Albert's reaction. If she's going to give it all that welly."

"I'll give it what I want. It's my bloody swan song."

"Keep your tits on. Sort it out later, if there's time," said the voice, and trilled out, "Take five!"

Kenneth took off his Inspector's hat and, with his long experience of studio protocol for bit-part players, waited to see whether the leading lady was going for a coffee, in order that he might not push ahead of her in the queue. Or he could ingratiate himself by buying her a cup? But she was talking animatedly with a man with two bright red earrings, maybe her agent, and showed no signs of wanting to move from the property divan. Kenneth turned away, took his smartphone from the breast pocket of his Inspector's uniform and tapped in to Messages. He was supposed to be meeting his beloved that night and hoped she had contacted him. But she had not.

As he put it back into his pocket, he felt a hand on his arm and looked down into the eyes of the man in the khaki tee shirt.

"I think I might have something for you. When can you and I have a little talk?"

Kenneth was used to receiving offers of work in unusual places; once in a bar on the Isle of Wight, once strapped to a seat in a Ferris wheel, and once when he and Helen were visiting a National Trust property in Derbyshire. The tough-guy actor would have plenty of good connections. He not only played the regular part of Albert in this soap, but also had his own TV series in which, with the help of various bald stand-ins, he undertook 'extreme' physical challenges supposedly set by the viewing public. Occasionally he played hairless hoodlums in low budget gangster films.

"Now would be a good time," said Kenneth, in answer to the other's question. "I'm free now. Unless they're going to reshoot that – "

"Nah. They won't do that. They'll do madam saying goodbye to the neighbours. They won't want us. Come on." He led Kenneth across the studio floor and down a brightly-lit corridor into a single dressing room which smelled unpleasantly of air freshener. "This is mine," he said gruffly, leading the way inside, shutting the door and clicking on the mirror lights.

They stood and faced each other in silence. A short bald man in a khaki tee shirt and a taller one, better-looking but incongruously dressed in a Police Inspector's uniform. After a brief pause the khaki-shirted one smiled, bent forward and touched the other in a manner that was quite unequivocal. As was the taller one's reaction. He jerked his knee up sharply into the other's groin, slammed him backwards into the dressing room wall, hissed "effing pervert!" into his face and left him doubled up on the floor.

He clicked off the mirror lights, opened and shut the dressing room door behind him and walked back into the studio, his mind churning. As the mists slowly cleared, he began to consider the implications of what he had just done.

In the short-term at least his loss of control might not prove too disastrous. He was fairly certain the bald queer would not make waves on the set – after all, it wouldn't do Baldy's reputation as a tough guy any good, would it? He felt momentarily consoled but still felt a tug of apprehension in case news of his hatred of that sort became widely known and did long-term damage to his standing in the business. A business in which abusing gays was still considered a worse crime than abusing women.

He was partly mollified when a few minutes later Baldy casually strolled back in to the studio and parked himself with his script on a canvas chair, without saying anything to anyone.

Upon which, like the thoroughgoing professional that he was, Kenneth stilled his daemon, repositioned his inner self within the essentially peace-loving nature of Inspector Bull, re-checked his script and put all thoughts of bigotry and violence completely out of his mind.

Tonight, Inspector Bull would tell Kenneth's lover what had happened. He knew she would understand.

And would sympathise.

* * *

Strangely enough, it was Harris who finally put the murder investigation on the right track. Not because of a brilliant piece of lateral thinking, but because of a slice of luck.

That year in the South East, the first two weeks of January were bitter cold. In the coffee shops, as they warmed their hands on their cups, customers told tales of iced-up garage doors and the difficulties they had experienced in scraping the frost from their windscreens. In the street acquaintances asked each other whether they considered it cold enough for them, adding a rueful rider to the effect that global warming was not what it was. Bus timetables, intended to stand as models of metronomic accuracy, now contained only the faintest approximation to the truth. Bus shelters, formerly havens of calm, were now bubbling cauldrons of uncertainty, as intending passengers asked each other whether this or that number bus had already gone and what denomination might now be expected to appear.

Up on the Downs, despite the roads being regularly gritted, lay the carcasses of several cars, abandoned after failing to make it along the undulating roadways. High above them, deprived of their usual sources of nourishment, seagulls screamed their victimhood against the lowering grey skies. But on the frost-bitten grass below the sheep had fared better, and were huddled in straw bale pens, specially erected for them in the sheltered folds of the hills.

Traffic on the roads fared badly, but the train services fared even worse. Since the Second World War the passenger service to and from Eastbourne and its neighbours had been something of a liability to its tourist trade. For several decades, rail travel to and from the town had involved trains splitting, pointless changes of platform and random cancellations. But that Winter the service had, incredibly, got even worse. A combination of inept management, union action and freezing weather had knocked it flat. Lines which in the hot summer had merely buckled now twisted themselves into sailor's knots as the frost struck them. Power cables akin to those which kept the Trans/Siberian expresses running to time capitulated completely when faced with an English Winter in which temperatures sometimes sank as low as minus four degrees Celsius.

Drivers, signalmen and guards found themselves unable to turn up for work because they had been unable to navigate a route through the travel chaos they had helped to create. As a result, crewless trains stood immobile at major stations. When their journey finally did get under way passengers could still find themselves stranded in frost-bound countryside as their train crews waited in vain for clearance from an empty or inexpertly manned signal box. Having had to contend over the years with floods, sunshine, the wrong kind of snow and the screaming horror of leaves on the line, a spell of frosty weather appeared finally to have done for the railways.

On a Monday morning in January, on the London-bound platform of Polegate Station, a few miles out of Eastbourne, a disconsolate huddle of would-be passengers were looking at their smartphones, stamping their fur-lined boots and peering down the line in the forlorn hope of seeing an approaching train.

The opposite platform, on to which passengers from London disembarked and on which commuters into Eastbourne waited was, by contrast, empty.

Which did not mean there was nobody waiting to board the Eastbourne train, should one arrive. It only meant that while they waited would-be travellers had sensibly taken refuge in the warmth of Derek Bowskill's newspaper shop across the station concourse.

They were standing there now, flicking through the colourful magazines on display and buying chocolate bars to mitigate the ordeal of the eight-minute journey into Eastbourne. They expected to be forewarned of the arrival of the London train by the crossing gates, just by the station, clanging shut.

Yet before the crossing gates sounded something quite extraordinary occurred. Two or three of the passengers in Bowskill's shop were looking across to the station when they saw a girl in a white mackintosh suddenly appear. There she was, in a blink, standing with her back to the station wall. Her appearance was so sudden that spectators told each other jokingly they didn't know whether she had materialised out of a manhole cover or had been dropped there from a passing spaceship.

Then the laughter froze on their lips because, as they watched, the girl's legs suddenly buckled beneath her and she collapsed in a heap on to the asphalt.

At once they rushed out to her aid. Willing hands lifted her bag from beneath her inert form, her legs were laid flat, her head cradled in anxious arms. But she gave no sign of life. Worried, they decided to carry her across to the warmth of Bowskill's shop. Was she suffering from the cold, from a rogue virus or was she simply drunk? The sickly-sweet smell which hung about her gave the lie to all three. This slim and beautiful girl with the classically chiselled features who had appeared from nowhere in a white Burberry Mackintosh was stoned out of her mind.

"That smell," said Bowskill, "God in Heaven!" Then added oafishly, "I don't want her dying in here. I've seen enough trouble. I'm ringing the police, now."

So he did. And some put it down to providence, others to pure chance, but Sergeant Harris at that time was being driven out to Stone Cross by a young constable. He happened to be passing Polegate as Bowskill rang HQ. As it was an emergency and as he was in the area, Harris' driver was told to respond.

The car was there inside four minutes.

After a quick examination of the girl's prostrate form, Harris turned to Bowskill. "Have you rung for an ambulance?"

"Yes. They said eight minutes." Holding it at arm's length in front of him, "Do you want to look through her bag?"

Harris took it gingerly. Gingerly sniffed it. Then shook his head. Best done in the lab. He explained to the young Constable that he intended to travel with the girl in the ambulance. The youngster presumed that his superior was proposing this because the patient might die in transit and that involved a lot of paper work.

But there was in fact another reason.

Harris had recognised the girl.

*　*　*

On Wednesday, there was a snowstorm. The trains became even scarcer and up on the Downs the gritting lorries were losing their battle with the elements. In Lewes Julia Jackson-Grant swallowed her pride and asked for a police car and driver to take her into work.

In Alfriston the pubs and teashops were all but empty. The tourists were waiting for warmer weather and the flood of ghoulish sightseers who had daily invaded the village following Colonel Baxter's barbaric despatch had slowed to a trickle.

In one of the thinly inhabited pubs on the High Street Mrs Moon and Gretchen the barmaid were catching up on the latest gossip about the murders. Among the locals there was no settled view. Some blamed Vladimir Putin. Others knew for a fact that it was all a put-up job by the Eastbourne Tourist Department, anxious to promote their town with as racy an image as that enjoyed by Brighton. Even less plausibly, another group explained that the disfiguring of the corpses was down to a blood-maddened gorilla that had broken out from a secret laboratory in Drusilla's, the local, highly-esteemed, children's zoo.

"What do yow think it is?" asked Gretchen warily. She had a limited stock of imagination and it had already been stretched to the limit by the highly fanciful theories that customers had offered over recent weeks.

"Drugs," said Mrs Moon, succinctly.

"Oi heard that, an' all" said Gretchen, relieved that Mrs Moon's theory, though absurd, at least involved no flying saucers, time travel or Witches' Sabbaths. Though you could never be quite sure about the funny lady with the long fingernails. She had crystal balls and green men and straw dollies and all sorts of clobber displayed in her shop. And there had been rumours that under the cover of night she had been visited by strange men.

"Did you hear about that actress that they found stuffed up with crack at Polegate Station?" asked Gretchen, cleverly changing the subject before Mrs Moon could bang on and on about her boring theory.

"Yes, I did."

"I've heard she had something to do with it. What do yow think?"

"I don't see how she could have. She was in a play in London all through December"

"How do yow know that?"

"It was in the *Telegraph*. They reviewed the play. Said she was outstanding, a distinctive new talent."

Temporarily outmanoeuvred, Gretchen asked her whether the *Telegraph* had anything about the battered old van they'd found after Christmas in the rocks under Beachy Head? The barmaid added there'd been a photograph of it in the *Herald* and the Editor had asked on the front page whether it was the murder van! Did Mrs Moon have anything to say about that?

She did. "You mustn't believe everything you read in the papers," Mrs Moon said. (Well, what about the newspapers saying that crackhead woman had been in a play in London then? Gretchen thought.)

Anyway, Mrs Moon then said she'd heard from another source that the winter tides had washed that van so clean it wasn't any use now to forensics. Gretchen had no reply to that as she didn't really know who forensics were.

She would perhaps have done better to ask Mrs Moon why that lady was so absolutely certain that drugs were the cause of the Moorland murders?

* * *

Helen was put straight in to Intensive Care. She had policewomen on guard by her bedside twenty-four hours a day. By Friday she seemed to have recovered sufficiently for her to be moved out and placed in a single ward, but the police guard remained on duty.

At four o' clock that afternoon she was visited by Inspector Plover, who quietly drew up a plastic stacking chair at her bedside. WPC Pollard stood sentinel at the foot of the bed.

She half opened her eyes and stared up at him.

"Miss Wittington, my name is Philip Plover. I'm an Inspector in the East Sussex Police Force. I hope you feel able to talk to me."

A barely audible whisper, "Yes."

"And I hope you are now feeling a little better. You've been very ill. We were really quite alarmed for you."

"Bit better."

"Good. Well this will not be a long visit. Other colleagues will want to talk with you when you feel up to it."

Almost a sigh, "Yes."

"Thanks to my sharp-eyed sergeant, who watches television a good deal, when you fell ill in the forecourt of Polegate Station, he recognised you immediately. We learned that until last year you lived in Eastbourne. We also learned that you're an actress and in the public eye. So, I want you to know that while you're in the hospital we shall make it our business to see that the reporters don't bother you. And anything you tell us remains confidential, unless it becomes necessary to disclose it to a court of law."

A faintly audible breath.

"What we want to know is, why were you carrying an opened packet of hard drugs in your bag? I'm told that they had a very high street value. Why they were in your possession? And why you were in the Station forecourt?"

There was no answer. Plover continued in the same measured tone.

"I'm going to tell you a little story. Once upon a time in the city of London there lived a gang of very rich drug barons. The police strongly suspected them, but they were too clever to be caught. These rich barons decided that they would divert suspicion from themselves by opening up drug dealerships in a few provincial towns or cities. And one of the places they picked was Eastbourne. They chose it because it was really the last place the police would think of. Like everybody else the police thought of Eastbourne as a retirement home for harmless old folk. That's what people think of Eastbourne, isn't it?"

Her features were impassive.

"However," Plover continued, "there was one big difficulty for the London barons. How could they convey the drugs to the dealers? How to get those valuable packets safely carried down from Knightsbridge to Eastbourne? The faces of the barons were well known to the police. So were the faces of their minders. And all the trains and buses going down to the South Coast were being watched. The barons needed carriers who were going down to Eastbourne for a perfectly legitimate reason and who wouldn't be suspected. Are you with me so far?"

Again, no response.

"Eventually, they hit on a solution. Eastbourne still has two or three old theatres who put on shows with live actors in them. You'd know about that, being in the business. So, why not use live actors as their carriers? From the barons' point of view the actors' merit was that usually they are only down here for a few days.

"The carriers are very well-paid – but you know that already. The barons call this method of distributing drugs 'going to the country'. There's very little risk attached to it. The carrier doesn't even have to deliver the package directly to the dealer – too risky. No, all he or she has to do is to go into a car park at a stated time and slip the package into a car bearing the number plate which the carrier is told to look out for.

"By the way we found the car number for your little enterprise printed on a sheet of notepaper in your bag. The car you were expecting was there waiting for you in the Polegate Station car park on Monday morning, wasn't it?"

No response.

"I hope you'll be able to supply the ending to my little story. Think about it very carefully. One of my colleagues will be here to see you tomorrow morning to ask you a few more questions. Good night and sleep well."

Helen spent the night time hours wading through dark waters and hearing over and over the Inspector's echoing voice until the early morning crash of the tea trolley in the corridor intruded into her consciousness and she fell into a deep sleep. Thereafter they repeatedly woke her to ask whether she would like tea or coffee, whether she would take her pills, have a wash, choose a cereal for breakfast, buy a newspaper and then, just as she was drifting off again, whether she would receive a visitor?

The nurses fluffed up her pillows, drew her upright and arranged a chair by her bed. It seemed her visitor was important.

Yet the lady who entered looked anything but important - middle-aged, sensibly dressed for the weather, her hair neatly combed in a bun, like a primary schoolteacher. But that judgement had to be modified when she sat down and reached out her hand to touch Helen. For some reason the lady had let her hails grow long, dangerously long, like talons on a bird of prey.

But Helen did not live to converse with the curious Mrs Moon. Even as her visitor was settling herself down, she had imperceptibly slipped from a state of mere unconsciousness into the Halls of Eternal Rest.

SIX

As soon as they had settled themselves around his desk Plover opened proceedings.

"Today Mrs Jackson-Grant is unable to chair our meeting because she has had to attend a police commissioners' conference up in London – "

"Is that why you've called it for this morning?" asked Dickinson, provoking a few wry grins around the room. Plover's growing antipathy to Julia Jackson-Grant had not gone unnoticed.

"I have called it because we've received the Coroner's report on Helen Wittington's body. Her death, it appears, was indeed down to a massive drugs overdose. Whether the drugs were self-administered, which seems unlikely, or pumped into her by somebody else, we do not yet know. If it was somebody else, we haven't got a name yet. Meanwhile, we've put out an appeal for anyone in this area who knew her to come forward.

"Now it seems likely that her death is related to our investigation. So, I thought it a good time for us to meet up, consider what we've got, move the pieces around and see if we can't discern a pattern."

"Let's hope so," from Dimmock, "Let's give it a crack."

"Which is a good moment to introduce our distinguished visitor." Plover indicated a newcomer to the murder team, a placid-looking middle-aged lady seated at one corner, a pale blush on her cheeks, hands clasped modestly on her lap beneath the desktop. "It is my pleasure to introduce Detective Inspector Moon from the Metropolitan Drugs Squad, who has been working in this area under deep cover for some little time. DI Moon made herself and her work known to me a few weeks ago, after PC Fletcher's murder. As you will hear, her investigations link up with ours."

"*August Moon*!" cried WPC Pollard, "That little shop in Alfriston. I recognise you now!"

"That's me," said the lady, adding unsmilingly, "you've blown my cover. Clever you."

Pollard blushed slightly and looked down at her thumbs.

"This morning we're going to go over a lot of old ground," said Plover, "and some new. I want to make sure that everyone speaks their mind, so there will be no official record kept."

"Can we take personal notes?" Harris asked.

"Of course, but no smartphones. First, I'll ask Detective Inspector Moon to speak."

In a voice much sharper than the one she had used as a village shop keeper, Moon began, "There's no call for you to know the ins and outs of the London end, but we got wind more than a year ago that some ugly customers in London, big drug chiefs, were branching out and setting up dealerships in places you don't normally associate with serious crime, or with serious drug use: Hereford, for instance, the Cotswolds, Durham ... and Eastbourne."

"Plenty of drugs here already," Dickinson said.

"Look at the clubs," added Harris.

"I'm not talking a few cheap pushers," said Moon. "I'm talking big drugs, big money. I'm talking about a drugs business that doesn't just serve the kids in the South East but links up through Gatwick to Continental Europe, Canada, America, anywhere in the world. A multi-million-pound business."

A ripple of doubt. "Listen up," said Plover sharply, "to what DI Moon has to say."

"My brief down here," she went on, "was to get a handle on the South East part of the organisation. Whoever was storing and distributing the stuff. They've got all sorts of systems in place to keep the names of the top people secret. But me and my assistant reckon that we've cracked it,"

"Your assistant?" queried Dimmock.

"Inspector Murray – 'my son Graham'," said the Inspector. "It's a double act. We've done it before."

A puzzled silence.

"Well, aren't you going to tell us," Dimmock burst out, "who the big chief is?"

"It's a complicated answer. If you just want the name of a local drug pusher then what about a gentleman who is no longer with us? Colonel Richard Broadribb Baxter, of Iris Cottage, Alfriston."

Looks were once more exchanged. "That old man? Drug dealer?" said Harris disbelievingly. "So, was that why he was killed?" from somebody else.

"No," said Moon briskly, "that wasn't the reason he was killed. I know it wasn't the London boys who killed him and it most certainly wasn't the Met. The killer is someone who wanted Baxter out of the way. Who is now the big chief in this area …"

"Do you know who that is?"

"We think we do. But we're not giving you a name until we've truly nailed the bastard."

"Let's switch focus," said Plover quickly. "What do we know of Baxter's background?"

"Local boy," said Dimmock, "Eastbourne College, then Downing College, Cambridge. Read English. Got a 2:1. Then a long army career. Tours of duty in Cyprus and Far East. Served with distinction in Afghanistan. After retiring to Alfriston he volunteered as a Neighbourhood

Constable and helped train cadets. Served as a sidesman in his local church, did several broadcasts about his main hobby, which was birdwatching. Member of Friends of Devonshire Park and Friends of the Royal Hippodrome, President of Ornithological Society. Unmarried – "

"Stop right there," said Plover. "Sergeant Harris noticed something important when he went to interview Baxter the morning after Fletcher's body was discovered. Harris?"

"In his dining room," said Harris, "he had the official police photograph of Keith Fletcher. It was mounted in a silver frame. That means he must have known him before it all kicked off. There wouldn't otherwise have been time to – anyway why should he – "

"Why should he?" echoed Plover. "So, what was the link between Baxter and Fletcher?"

"Baxter was gay. We know that. Could Fletcher have been... ?"

"Possible," Plover said. "But Baxter must have had other boyfriends, and their photographs weren't on display. Fletcher must have been important to Baxter in some other way."

"Drugs?" somebody suggested. "Could Fletcher have been working for Baxter?"

"No!" Moon cut in sharply. "We've got the drug operation well in our sights, including the barons and the mules. Fletcher wasn't even on the radar. From everything I've learned about him, I'd say it was very unlikely that he even used drugs."

"OK, let's leave that for the moment," Plover was anxious to avoid cul-de-sacs. "Weigh up what we know about the murders themselves. Opportunity and motive. We know Baxter was lured in to the empty shop premises and killed, almost certainly by having his throat slashed. The body was then - no other word for it – disembowelled, taken to the theatre, dressed in a nightgown and tied to the magic beanstalk so that his corpse was displayed to the whole theatre audience. The question is, why?"

For a moment nobody spoke. The memory of that dangling flesh was too close to them.

Eventually Dickinson volunteered, "As some kind of warning?"

"But who to? And why was Fletcher's body exhibited in a public place? Same questions. Same brick wall. We know nothing incriminating about him. Born in Sheffield. Three brothers. Did quite well at school, then joined the Police Cadets and graduated to the Force. Was sent down here a few months ago. Ambitious. He'd started to do an Open University Degree. No obvious vices. Like I said to his parents at the funeral, he was destined for great things. I can't think why anybody would have wanted to seek Fletcher out and – "

"Disfigure him," put in Dimmock tactfully.

"And disfigure him – exactly. It's likely that the same person – or persons – killed Fletcher and Baxter. Both bodies were exhibited after death. And both were - mutilated. But not in the same way, or at the same site. There was no trace of Fletcher found in the shop premises. So far, we haven't even established where he was shot, nor where his face was smashed in like that."

"No progress on the van found under Beachy Head?" Dimmock asked.

"The sea water had washed everything out of it and scoured off any prints. That's been established." Moon sounded impatient with provincial investigators who couldn't keep up.

"So far as Fletcher is concerned," Plover said, "the problem we still have to answer is why did he keep his police uniform on that night?" DI Moon closed her eyes in apparent exasperation. "So, come on everybody, think!! Throw out a few ideas! Nobody's going to judge you."

Answers came in a rush. "Trying to impress a girl?" "Impress a boy?" "Doing a bit of overtime?" "Having his portrait done?" "Lost his memory?" "His other clothes were in the wash?"

Invention then began to falter, threatening to burn out completely.

At that moment, a radical new idea, too dangerous to mention to his serving colleagues, presented itself to Plover. An altogether shocking possibility.

Which had been staring him in the face for weeks.

He started and looked around him, momentarily ashamed of having allowed his intuition to take over his conscious mind.

But no, his colleagues were still frowning with the effort of brainstorming and had noticed nothing.

And Detective Inspector Moon was still rocking back on her chair with her eyes tight shut, oblivious to everyone else in the room.

* * *

Soosie looked down breathlessly on Kenneth's prostrate form. "You went at me like a pile driver, man. What is it with you today?"

"What do you mean?"

"It was all about getting yourself off, wasn't it? I might as well have been a blow-up doll."

"You wanted to visit this afternoon."

"Course I did, but if I'd known you were going to behave like that, I'd have stayed at home."

"Behave like what?"

"You know what I'm saying. You even stopped lookin' at me straight. Is it because of this drugs business with your old girl friend?"

"With Helen? No, it isn't. Like I told you, she's been out of my life for months. She was nothing to me."

Soozie arched herself upright and looked down at him accusingly. "It seems to me that just now you were trying to get rid of Helen. Trying to knock her out of your system. Christ!" she added, remembering Kenneth's roughness.

"You've been sleeping in a single bed too long."

"Don't you try blaming me! No, Kenny, there's no two ways about it, it's down to you. When I first knew you, you were a great lover. You liked me to have a good time, didn't you? Now - oh man - you're just out for number one. Haven't your other lady friends complained?"

"No, they haven't complained." He did not choose to mention just how few of his other lady friends he was currently seeing. Though it was true that she hadn't complained.

He hurried on, "But yes, you're quite right. There is another reason. I'll tell you what it is. A few days ago I shot a couple of scenes in that soap thing. You know, set round that Birmingham pub. I was the one who arrested Ariadne for murder." Soozie nodded. "Well, I was expecting to play the same character in the trial scenes they're shooting in February. Then this morning my agent got a message saying they've written my character out. Apparently, I'm not wanted."

"You're saying that's the reason you're in this mood?"

"Yes, that's the reason."

"And it's not because of Helen dying?"

"I give you my word."

"Why don't the TV people want you then?"

"I don't know," said Kenneth, who darkly suspected that the bald queer who played Albert had a lot to do with it. "It's a chancy business, television. In television, it's a case of who you know, rather than whether you're any good."

"You get that everywhere Kenny. I get that in the supermarket. From top management."

"Sorry to hear it."

They each stood up and began to dress. Kenneth was trying to convince himself that Soozie now believed that his dark mood was solely because of a professional snub.

Soozie, as she slowly pulled on her jeans, did not believe a word of it. She had a fair notion of what the actual cause might be. The only question was, with whom should she share her suspicions?

* * *

As the Jaguar idled in Upperton Road, waiting in the lunchtime traffic for the lights to change, Clifford noticed a familiar blue people carrier going in the opposite direction, then turning off towards Old Town. Julia's off to *The Lamb* for a business lunch, he said to himself.

It was still freezing cold but only faint traces of winter were now visible. A thin covering of snow still etched patterns on the Meads rooftops and frost had bleached the remaining colour out of the Downs.

Clifford turned into the Avenue and slotted the Jaguar neatly into its allotted space by the side of his office. Here there remained little evidence of the recent snowfalls. Just that thin grey slush, compounded of salt, sand and dirty water, that seems to cover every flat surface in the UK when the snows depart.

Though the office car park had been swept it was still wet and gritty underfoot. Ever fastidious, Clifford covered the ground between his heated car and the heated porch in four loping strides, pausing when inside the door to clean his shoes in the ancient brushing mechanism in the hallway. He was about to enter his office when Miss Foster popped out of her lair to tell him he had a visitor.

"Who is it, Miss Foster?"

The Secretary was equal to that. "Kenneth Molloy," she read from her pad.

"Has he got an appointment?"

"No, Mr Mollison, he has not got an appointment." Clifford knew what was coming. "I cannot make appointments unless you keep your diary up to date. I told him I thought you would be in before lunch, and he's been waiting for you. He didn't want to see anybody else. But if it's not convenient I can make an appointment for next week. That is, if you tell me when you are coming in."

It was a long-standing bone of contention. Clifford, Senior Partner in the firm, retained only a few well-to-do families as clients and passed all the new business to his younger, more biddable colleagues. He otherwise spent his time in some of the customary pursuits of the well-to-do Eastbourne male – golf, drinking, bridge, bird watching, the Masons and the occasional trip to London to attend imaginary conferences. He had no intention of revealing details about any of these activities to his secretary and hence to the chattering classes of Eastbourne. "I'm so sorry Miss Foster," he said in mock contrition, "I'll try to do better. And, of course I'll see Mr Molloy. What does he do?"

"Classical and contemporary. And character roles."

"He's an actor?"

"He is."

"Oh my God. Well, wheel him in."

Whatever expectations Clifford may have had of Kenneth Molloy, they were immediately dispelled by his appearance. He had none of that bleached, pale-blue, rakish look which male actors usually cultivate offstage.

Instead the man before him could well have been taken for a well-to-do solicitor. He was neatly and expensively dressed, even down to wearing polished shoes with gold buckles and sporting a striped club tie. And he strode in confidently – in contrast to most first-time visitors who entered the office diffidently, cowed by the wide vista of polished desk and the ornate framed photograph of Clifford with his arm around most of his wife that hung on the panelled wall behind him. Upon which, Clifford noticed, his visitor's eyes had come to rest.

"My wife Gwen and I," Clifford said, "on holiday in Sardinia."

"Indeed," said Kenneth, wrenching his eyes from the portrait and accepting a leatherette seat opposite the Solicitor. "Your wife and you on holiday. Indeed. Sloth. Indeed. Well now," he said, preparing to play the role of interlocutor, "I expect you'd like to know why I'm here."

Clifford intimated that he would like that.

"You were particularly recommended to me by Mrs Jackson-Grant."

"Ah, yes, Julia," said Clifford, implying an intimacy between the lady and himself which Kenneth knew was unjustified. If this had been a film he would at this point have looked askance at Mollison, cocked his trilby, stretched back in his chair, laconically rolled a cigarette and murmured, 'So - tell me all you know about Julia'. As it was, realising that while he was fantasising the

Solicitor had been asking something, Kenneth said, "I'm so sorry. Could you say that again?"

"I said, do you know Ben?"

"Ben?"

"Julia's husband, Ben. Inspector Jackson-Grant."

"Yes, of course. Of course I do. Though not as well as I know Julia."

Clifford thought this odd but put it aside and asked if there was anything else Kenneth wanted to say.

Kenneth said there was and, with admirable brevity, set out his grievances against the television company. Was there any chance, he asked, of successfully suing them for constructive dismissal?

"Not a hope," said the lawyer, which brisk professional opinion did not seem to disturb Kenneth in the slightest. He thanked Clifford for his time, shook hands and politely took his leave.

Alone, the Solicitor fell to wondering what had been the real reason for his visit? What had Kenneth been intending to ask him? And what had made him change his mind?

SEVEN

Brenda Barnaby kept strictly to the formula she had agreed with Plover. She passed on the names of all those people who signed up to her Vigilantes Group - though it had to be admitted that recruitment had, since Christmas, rather fallen away. In return Inspector Plover had continued to brief the MP on (parts of) the inquiry's progress and regularly assured her that arrests were imminent. What Plover had not done however was to tell her how her civil volunteers could meantime be of use, for there was no denying that the lack of action had led to a certain restlessness in the ranks.

Today Mrs Barnaby was conducting her Saturday Clinic, her lank form hunched into the back room of the shop premises which served as the Party's office. The thin trickle of dissatisfied constituents having been successfully staunched, a relaxed Brenda was now allowing herself the luxury of thinking private thoughts. The big question she debated with herself was, should she disband the Vigilantes? Dare she admit that one of her well-publicised initiatives, ostensibly undertaken on behalf of her constituents, had been nothing more than a cheap political gesture? It would take guts. The other campaigns she had led – to attract a John Lewis store into the town, to bring back the sand to local beaches, to restore the train timetables to their pre-war reliability – had also been vote-pulling stunts of course, but the crucial difference was that they had no time limit set for their completion. If political opponents asked about them Mrs Barnaby was always able to say she was still in there, pitching.

The recent murder inquiry on the other hand existed within a certain time frame. If the killer was exposed in the near future, the police would naturally take the credit. Barnaby would not be able to proclaim, as was her usual habit, that this desirable outcome was down to her selfless diligence. On the other hand, if the killings remained unsolved for some time, the whole sequence of events would morph into one of those great unsolved British mysteries so beloved of folklorists, and her Eastbourne Vigilantes would be remembered, if at all, as a risible footnote to failure.

The door to her room opened and Councillor Muttley poked her scrawny head round it to tell her she had another customer. She then opened the door wide so that the newcomer – a burly lady of colour – could squeeze past her through the door. The MP stood up, switched on her smile of welcome and motioned her to a chair on which the visitor sat awkwardly, overawed by the bright crimson and yellow poster, '*Barnaby gets Whitehall buzzing*' which adorned the wall behind the desk.

"I'm not sure this is the right place …" she began.

Barnaby pulled on her 'Your MP is now deigning to listen to you, insignificant mortal' face, pushing her gold-rimmed spectacles right down to the end of her beaky nose in a way that she hoped made her look wise but kindly, like God. "That all depends on what you want to know," she said encouragingly. "I find I can help with most things. If I can't, I can almost certainly recommend someone who can." She topped this off with a medium-grade smile. So, what was this woman's problem? If Brenda were laying a bet, she'd have put money on it being some legal quibble about her dwelling place. Some argument about extending a lease perhaps – that was a regular difficulty in Eastbourne. Or maybe she'd come about the rough sleepers and lager louts who infested the promenade in the evenings ..."

"I want to talk about that woman in Polegate Station, who died of the drugs overdose," her constituent said abruptly.

"You should talk to the police," said Mrs Barnaby. And instantly regretted it. "After we've discussed your problem," she added lamely. It may be that this lady's story might be the spur to get her Vigilantes pitched into the action at last. She pasted on her most imposing smile, the one which accompanied a winsome little twitch of her cheek muscles, leant back encouragingly and said, "Do tell."

"Well, my name is Soozie Wade. I live on Priory Lane, near the football ground. It's about my boyfriend, Kenneth Molloy. What it is, he used to live with Helen Wittington, the girl who collapsed by Polegate Station. He was ..."

"One moment," said Barnaby, "Do the police know this? That your boyfriend used to live with her?"

"What? Oh, yes of course they know. Kenny went to see them as soon as he heard she'd died."

"She wasn't down here to visit him?"

"No. He didn't know she was in the area. That's what I'm saying. They only gave out her name after she passed. And put her photograph on the television. That's when Kenny realised. And, of course, he went straight to the police."

"Quite right," nodded Barnaby, "Quite right. But I don't quite see ..."

"That's what I'm saying. Since he heard about Helen and the drugs and that, he's been a changed man. Like a caged lion. And he's got violence in him. No doubt about that. I think if he ever finds out who did that to Helen, he'll kill them. I'm worried for him ..."

Her voice tailed off.

There was no denying that Barnaby was disappointed by Soozie's disclosure. Nothing there for the Vigilantes to get their teeth into. Trying to purge her voice of the regret she felt, she said,

"Well, Miss Wade, I must advise you to communicate your anxieties to the police."

"Whatever you say."

And when Soozie did, she found them much more receptive. She spoke first to a Sergeant Harris, who listened patiently to what she had to tell him, nodded a great deal then passed her on to his boss, Inspector Plover, who seemed very interested indeed. Unlike Harris and Mrs Barnaby, Plover wanted to know exactly how her boyfriend had displayed his anger.

When she'd told him, he seemed very concerned to establish the exact date of their joyless lovemaking. And before that, when was the last time they'd made love? Plover raised his eyebrows when she told him that, but he made no comment.

And Soozie said no more about it. If Inspector Plover wanted to believe Kenny and she were satisfied with sex once every three weeks, she could have no objection.

But Plover was a skilled interrogator and knew when to press and when to relax the pressure. He said nothing further about their lovemaking but chatted in more general terms. Soon Soozie had revealed not just the name but also the address of the man she called her boyfriend.

And within fifteen minutes of her departure Plover's team had matched the information with the name and address of the man who had been advertising himself as a prospective companion to local women 'of all ages'.

* * *

Things now began to move more quickly. Plover decided that there was only one person with whom he could possibly share his sudden insight into the identity of the killer. At first he had considered several other people for the role of confidant. Harris he rejected at once, not because he had any doubts about his ability to keep it all under his hat, but because he was probably incapable of the lateral thinking which this case required. Detective Inspector Moon, who might have been ideal for his purpose, seemed to have gone to earth and had rendered herself incommunicado. Mollison he didn't like and Julia was plainly unsuitable in this context. Yet he must talk it over with someone who would not simply assume that the strain was telling on him and that he had taken leave of his senses.

For a brief period Plover even considered breaking their house rule and sharing his theory with his partner, a lawyer. For several years the pair had operated on the understanding that neither would discuss details of the other's cases. But on reflection Plover decided that as his partner would know nothing of the people involved, there was no advantage in breaking their agreement.

Finally he decided there was only one person with whom he could share his thoughts. That was his old mentor, Ben Jackson-Grant.

A cautiously phrased telephone enquiry elicited the information that Ben would be happy to discuss the case with him. He had, it appeared, thoroughly considered every aspect of the crimes and was also close to a solution. However, whereas Plover had finally made an intuitive leap to the answer, Grant had worked methodically.

His invariable method was to use Occam's Razor, which stated that once you had excluded all the impossibilities, that which remains (however improbable it may seem) will be the correct solution.

The two had spoken warily, knowing how easily phones could be tapped. But they had worked together for many years. Though their talk was guarded they sensed they were working towards similar solutions.

They arranged to meet on the following Wednesday at three o' clock in the afternoon in a dingy hotel lounge in Lewes' main thoroughfare. Ben arranged for a specialised local taxi service, which had a cab capable of loading and disgorging his motorised wheelchair, to collect him at the back door of his home. He and Snuff got in and were conveyed to the rear door of the hotel, where Plover was waiting.

Although Plover had checked that the back room was accessible to wheelchairs and that the hotel accepted dogs, and although there did not seem to be anyone interested either in their movements or in their conversation, they still went through the pantomime of pretending they had met by the merest chance.

And when they had seated themselves and tea had been brought in, they still spoke cautiously. A casual bystander would have gained very little insight into the precise nature of their collaboration.

They agreed to meet again on the coming Friday afternoon at the Jackson-Grant residence.

But the person who heard this and who had recorded the rest of their conversation was most certainly not a casual bystander.

* * *

Outside *Zizzi's* workmen were engaged in digging up the pavements again, to better accommodate the new Temporary Bus Terminals (TBTs). Inside the restaurant Gwen Mollison watched for a few minutes while potential passengers groped their way around the maze of bollards, railings and cunningly disguised man traps, searching in vain for the new temporary TBTs.

Tiring of the spectacle, she turned back to the *Readers' Letters* page of last week's *Herald*, on which could be found letters complaining of the foolishness of the Borough Council. Gwen believed that writing to the local paper was an exercise in pure egotism, as the EBC had never been known to reply to criticism, however well-founded. She did not read any of the letters but ran her eyes over the signatures, in case she knew any of the writers and, on a suitably public occasion, could upbraid them for their unworldliness. It was far better to take direct action, she would say. It's no use writing letters, you must talk to the top people.

As a case in point, she was now waiting for her friend Barbara Muttley, with whom she had a weekly lunch. And was on her third gin and tonic. "I'm waiting for the Leader of the Council," she said, rather too loudly, to the girl who was hovering by her table with a hopeful order pad.

"Ah, here she comes!" she cried a few moments later, as Mrs Muttley's spare frame appeared in the restaurant doorway. Gwen snatched off her spectacles and bared her gleaming teeth in a welcoming smile.

"Hello, Gwen darling," said the Leader as she settled herself at the table, topping up her greeting with an impressive riff on her smoker's cough. "Barbara dearest," Gwen replied, as soon as the last shuddering spasm was safely concluded. "I've ordered you a Macallans. So, how goes it? Bad meeting?"

"Don't ask!" implored Mrs Muttley, and immediately answered. "Dreadful business. Long chinwag about the local kids peddling drugs. You wouldn't believe! We had a special report from somebody in the Met. "Oh, thank you," she added as her malt whisky came and, just as rapidly, went. "I'll have another of those," she added sternly, implying by her tone that unless she made her wishes crystal clear, the waitress would certainly bunk off for the afternoon and leave them to die of thirst.

Gwen had another one as well, and they ordered light lunches. Barbara told her some more about the meeting, including the unhelpful questions the Opposition had asked, because though they didn't know it, they'd be the majority party one day and then they'd realise that when you were in government you had to keep certain things quiet. "Certain things quiet," Gwen echoed, "You're so right." And for a moment was lost in her own thoughts.

"Well, what does Clifford think of them?" "Think of what?" said Barbara, smiling helpfully. "The murders," said Gwen, "Weren't you listening?" "Yesterday's nudes," responded Barbara, giggling. "There'll likely be another one," warned Barbara, "that Inspector from the Met says we must all be on our guard against it. Blow me Gwen, she had some flesh on her, that one." "News. Yesterday's news," said Gwen, "that's what I meant, not nudes." She giggled some more, "Freudian slip." "Well, what does Clifford think?" asked Barbara.

"What does he matter? He's just a man. Why don't you ask me what I think? We're not just their goods and cattles. We've a right to our own opinions."

"All right then. What's your opinion?"

"What's my opinion?" said Gwen. "What's my opinion?"

"Yes."

"I'd like to hear your opinion first. You're nearer the action than I am."

"Well I think it's the drugs. You knew that Colonel Baxter was one of the drugs barons, didn't you?"

"No, I didn't."

"Well he was. I think it's all to do with the drugs trade. I shouldn't be surprised if that policeman wasn't mixed up in it. Rival drug gang killed them, I shouldn't wonder. Ah, lovely," she went on as their lunches arrived.

They settled down to eat, and after a few minutes Barbara said, "Now come on Gwen, what do you think?"

"Well," Gwen spoke between forkfuls, "you know I'm a great fan of whodunnits? Inspector Morse. Hercule Poirot. Miss Marple. Ze leetle grey cells."

"Exactly. Though I don't get much time for reading in my job."

"Tell me about it. I know what it is to be busy. Good Lord, yes. No, I read in bed. There isn't much else to do there."

"Oh, come on! What's Clifford doing while you're reading?"

"Sod all. Snoring probably. Would you like another drink?"

"I'd better not. I've got another meeting at three. Oh, go on, then." A little pause while this further refreshment was ordered, delivered and sampled. "Come on now. Who done it then?"

"Well, in whodunnits the least likely person always turns out to be the villain. The murderer is the one person you never thought of suspecting – the man who discovers the body, the local priest, the lady running the local charity shop, or the police inspector who's leading the murder hunt. So, why not apply that principle to this case? If Miss Marple were sitting here now, who would she finger? It would be the character you least suspect."

"OK, well who do you think the least likely murderer is?"

With a rather contrived giggle, "Well - there's you for a start."

"I'm flattered. Am I the least likely killer on the whole South Coast?"

"No, but you're one of the least likely." Emphasising each name with a jab of her spoon. "There's You, Clifford of course. Brenda Barnaby. Inspector Plover. Sergeant Harris. Julia Jackson-Grant ..."

"Ben Jackson-Grant"

"Ben Jackson-Grant. And Dick Rodham."

"Who's he when he's at home?"

"Estate agent from out Newhaven way. He's a member of the Chamber of Commerce. Clifford dislikes him a lot. Oh, and Rodham thinks Clifford did it, by the way."

"There's no reason why an estate agent should murder anybody," said Barbara obscurely. "What about you? Why aren't you on the list? You're always saying you've got things to hide. I wouldn't put it past you, Gwen."

They chomped for a few moments in silence before Gwen said:

"If I were going to kill anybody, it wouldn't be Colonel Baxter. Or that poor police constable. I didn't know either of them."

"No. Neither did I. But you see, it'll be drugs at the heart of it."

"And neither of us does drugs. Well, not more than average."

"Speak for yourself. At least after this morning I know where to get them. Now look," she went on as the bill was delivered, upside down, on a white plate, "I insist on paying for this."

"It's my turn," Gwen protested.

"OK," said Barbara, having flipped the bill over and seen the rather daunting total, "if you insist, we'll split it two ways."

"I'll leave the tip then. Next week at the same time?"

"By then, who knows, we might know who done it."

"I do hope not. There'd be nothing left to talk about."

EIGHT

"I'll be late home tomorrow night," said Julia, pulling on her coat, "We'll just have something on our knees when I get in."

"OK," said Ben from behind the *Argus*. "What time will you be home?"

"Fridays I usually get away early. And then I'm going to see Kenneth of course. I should be back about half-seven, eight o' clock time."

"That's all right. Only Plod's coming to see me tomorrow afternoon. Wants to pick my brains about something. I expect he'll have gone by the time you're back."

"Do give him my regards." She walked meditatively towards the door, where she paused, then suddenly turned. "Ben, do you still think Plover is the right man for this job?"

He had no need to ask which job. "It's not for me to say. You must have agreed that the case be given to him. He reports to you."

"But you know him much better than I do. You were his boss for years and he trusts you."

"Has he done anything wrong?"

"Nothing that counts as wrong, no. But I hear things about him. He's not a team player."

"He's a loner. There's not many people he trusts."

"He doesn't trust me."

"I'll ask him what's eating him. And whatever it is, I'll get straight back to you."

"But will you?" She smiled for no reason.

There was a time, early in their marriage, when Julia had embraced her husband every time she parted from him. When he came home after the accident that had become a peck on the cheek. Now she acknowledged their parting solely by means of a little grunt, as she turned and went out of the kitchen. He heard the creak and thud of the back door and then the uncomplaining growl of the People Carrier's engine as, despite being left outside all night, it started first time. He listened to it move away down the drive.

For a while Ben sat in silence. He knew he was approaching the climactic moment of the case and he knew its resolution would hurt him in a number of ways. Nevertheless, he was resolved to follow Plover to the conclusion. That was what separated police work from ordinary social judgement.

His thoughts went back to the events which had made him choose crime detection as his career.

At his London Comprehensive Ben had been a better-than-average pupil, bright but also good at games, so he was in with both the arty and the sporting crowd. He was also a favourite with the girls, and at the age of fourteen had already acquired a regular girlfriend, Janet, by popular acclaim the fittest girl in their year.

Then, for the first time in his life, he found he was being victimised - threatened by unsigned, handwritten notes which appeared in his locker, threatening that he would be 'beaten up' or 'slapped' unless he stopped going with Janet. It was a new and shocking experience for someone who hitherto had so effortlessly found favour with his peers. Young men of a heroic nature might possibly have ignored the taunts and risen above the whole thing. Muscular types might have guessed who the culprit was and beaten them up. Sneaks would have probably just whinged to the House Mistress. The cowardly would almost certainly have played safe and given Janet up.

Ben did none of these things. Instead he pinned a large sheet of card to his bedroom wall and on it printed the names of pupils in the same year. Methodically, by marking against each suspect such things as opportunity (to slide the notes under his locker door), possible motives, the information they appeared to have about his relationship with Janet, coupled with a comparison of their handwriting with the offending notes, he whittled down the list of suspects until there was only one remaining – his best friend Jez, the very last person he would have suspected at the outset.

He remembered with a slight frisson of embarrassment how he had, by relentless questioning spread over several days, finally got Jez to confess. He had then set about punishing him. First, by shopping him to the school authorities. Second, by delivering a fully-illustrated dossier of his crimes to Jez's embarrassed parents. The end result was that Jez, by then a pariah, was removed to a different Tutor Group and inevitably the two boys lost contact. (And when, years later, Jez and Janet were married, it was equally inevitable that Ben would not be invited to their wedding.)

Had he acted wisely, all those years ago? He had no doubt that he had found the right culprit, but had he been justified in shaming his former friend so completely? Should personal allegiances never play a part in detective work? And if friendships must always be set aside in such circumstances, would it not be better for the police, the moral guardians of society, to avoid friendships altogether? To live apart from their kinfolk? Like monks.

Ben sighed, turned about and trundled down the corridor to his study where Snuff, under the bookcase, gave a gentle woof to indicate that, should the opportunity arise, he was available to be fondled, fussed over and fed. Ben, still lost in thought, for once ignored the dog. He reached down and unlocked the drawer in which his blue notebook was kept. He perused it carefully, checked his retirement watch and, on the dot, dialled a prearranged number.

"Hello. This is your old friend."

"Hello, old friend," said Plover from his car phone, "Are we still on for tomorrow?"

"We are. And there'll be time to do everything that has to be done. The lady of the house will be out until at least nineteen hundred hours."

"I have some news I must give you tomorrow, old friend. News I'm afraid you may not like,"

"You must do what you must do," said Ben. "Roger."

"Roger and out," said Plover, as his car drew up outside Barnaby's Campaign Headquarters.

He wanted to tell her that, finally, arrests really were imminent.

And she could disband her wretched Vigilantes.

* * *

In Alfriston that Thursday afternoon, in the cramped flat above the premises of *August Moon*, the proprietor (a.k.a. Detective Inspector Moon) is taking coffee with 'her son' Graham (a.k.a. Inspector Murray).

The two of them have been listening intently to a recording made of a conversation which had taken place the day before in the lounge of a Lewes hotel. It had been easy to find out where Plover and Jackson-Grant were meeting, harder to persuade the hotel manager that Inspector Murray had to give the room a security sweep. In the course of which Murray had planted a minute listening device, little bigger than a pin head.

Though Murray was not convinced the deception was necessary. "We're in close touch with them. Why do we have to trick colleagues?"

"Graham, you have a lot to learn. In this game you must always know more than everybody else"

"Well, we've both heard the recording. Are we any the wiser? Do we know more than they do?"

"Not yet, no. Go back to – ", consulting a stop watch on the table beside her, "- fifty-one minutes."

Murray set it up, and it ran again. They heard Plod telling Ben that he was going to call on the suspect on Thursday, the day before they had arranged to meet again. Ben in reply urged him 'not to rattle the man's cage'. Plod reassured him, adding that they'd been watching the man for more than a week, checking up on who the man was seeing.

Then followed a brief hiatus because, it appeared, Ben had spilled something from the tea tray.

"Again," ordered DI Moon. "Just that last bit."

"We've had tabs on Kenneth Molloy for the last two weeks. We'd like to know who's been visiting him."

Followed by the silence, then the crash, then the apology. Still unsure of what was interesting his superior, Murray made a suggestion:

"The dog has knocked something over on the tray?"

"No, that's not it. Listen! Jackson-Grant's apologising on his own behalf. He knocked it over. He was agitated because Plover's finding out who's visited Molloy. Jackson-Grant's embarrassed by that."

"Could it be Jackson-Grant himself that's done the visiting?"

"Nice one. But no. He's a prisoner in that chair. It takes him two days to organise a trip to the shops. More likely to be his wife."

"Why should she visit Molloy?"

"Oh, come on Graham! Why do men and women meet?"

"But she's the Assistant Commissioner. He's… ."

"In a wheelchair, poor lamb. That wheelchair shapes this case."

NINE

On that fateful Friday the temperature had risen slightly and with the slow thaw, people started to suffer from pent-up chills and colds. As they always did at such times, they told each other that there was a 'bug going around'. It was spoken of in the singular, as if it were the same bug moving in the same circular motion, irrespective of the fact that the symptoms were markedly varied and appeared at quite different times in different people.

Clifford Mollison for example had little more than a runny nose, a mild inconvenience which only came upon him on Friday, although his secretary Miss Foster had been off for a week with laryngitis. Nevertheless, the wiseacres in the solicitors' office chose to see these afflictions as manifestations of the same encircling virus All that in spite of the fact that even when they were both in the building, Miss Foster and her boss scarcely ever occupied the same office, let alone manoeuvred themselves into more intimate proximity.

Mrs Rodham was minding the counter at the Newhaven Estate Agents, although she had suffered all week from neuralgia which, without a shred of evidence, she blamed on her absent husband. Gwen Mollison was developing a cough, which she privately decided she must have caught from Barbara Muttley, who in turn was suffering from a sore throat which made her sound like somebody impersonating Winston Churchill and gave her pronouncements in the Council Chamber a new depth and authority. Plover had man flu and being an irascible patient, was being given a wide berth by his colleagues. Soozie was suffering from a stomach ache but chose to set an example to the till workers by still turning up for work. However, the till workers, fearful of being infected by Soozie, then stayed away in droves. The one shining exception to all this was Julia who, like her husband, had escaped contagion altogether.

Kenneth, suffering in Old Town, fully accepted that his dark mood and cracking migraine were not caused by any communal bug, but by his own life choices. He had been visited on the previous evening by Inspector Plover, who had said it was just a chat, but it was obvious the way things were going. He had woken with dread in his stomach.

Now he was breakfasting alone in his small kitchen, packets of paracetamol on his side plate, looking askance at the script for a voiceover on an ad that he had received in the morning post. Though he was glad of any sort of work, the script did not enthuse him. The product being puffed was a supermarket favourite, heavily advertised on TV - a knobbly-looking cereal bar smelling of washing-up liquid and the colour of baby sick. This script followed the well-tried formula of using a friendly animated cartoon character to excite the kiddies. In this case the alleged health-giving properties of the cereal bar were to be personified by a cross-eyed bullfrog who smirked suggestively and capered heavily about to the jingle:

> Put a smile upon your face,
>
> A flying start in every race,
>
> It's Ki – Ki – Kids own Krunchers!

Then, as the frog started to stuff its face with cereal bars, an authoritative voice-over (Kenneth?) was to say, "Wise mothers recommend Krunchers as the healthy way to start your day." Then in a jollier tone, "Just like Francis Frog's mum!" Quick shot of a transvestite frog wearing a cap and apron, tucking into yet more bars of congealed baby sick. It was to end with a close-up of the manufacturer's logo and Francis Frog jumping up and giving a 'thumbs up' sign.

It was all deeply repugnant to him, the nastiest possible insight into the sordid commercial world of child exploitation. His creative self cried out in horror when faced with such drivel, his moral self winced at its blatant materialism, his aesthetic self at its inexcusable vulgarity. But on the other hand, the fee for such work was, per hour, about ten times what he got for rehearsing and appearing in a stage play. Moreover, the job would be over in a day and afterwards he could forget all about it. Plus, there were no credits linking him to that vile excrescence. So, if anybody ever asked him if it was his voice on that horrible Krunchers advertisement, he could deny it hotly, claiming he would never, ever sink that low.

He reached over and signed the contract. And almost at once his dark mood began to lift. He had liberated his theatrical self, which was the translucent core of his being. He was an actor once more, playing a part – a moronic frog as it happened, but it was a part. He carefully set up his pocket voice recorder, then went over and over the same lines until he had the piece pitch-perfect, the rhythm of the jingle merging seamlessly with the brainless frog's dance:

"It's Ki – Ki – Kid's Own Krunchers!"

Sang Kenneth, as the morning wore on. Occasionally he essayed a jerky parody of the frog's weird capering. And when his smartphone rang, so immersed was he in the Kruncher universe that it was not Kenneth but Francis Frog who answered it:

"It's Ki-Ki-Kid's Own Crunchers! Hello to the Deputy Area Commander. Hello Julia. No, I'm not. Jober as a Sudge. I was simply rehearsing." There followed a stream of verbiage from the caller. "This afternoon? Of course, yes." More words. "I'm comfortable with that, Yes."

After the Deputy Commander had terminated the call, for a few moments Kenneth continued to stare fixedly at his phone, then slowly and reverently put it down on his kitchen table. He sat, head in his hands, while his high spirits once more trickled away to nothing. A Stygian Darkness enveloped him like a shroud.

And he knew the infinite pain of remorse - for that which is done ...

And cannot be undone.

* * *

By four o' clock on that Friday afternoon an icy rain had begun to fall. Julia parked, as she always did, a little way down the road from Kenneth's. Then she pulled on the cagoule she kept by her for such emergencies and half walked, half ran to the maisonette.

In a parked VW on the opposite side of the road Inspector Murray was trying out a card trick on Detective Inspector Moon. Alerted by her gaze, Murray turned and watched Julia pause in the porch and search for something in the pocket of her trousers.

Though she had a key Julia was in the habit of ringing the doorbell before she let herself in. She did so on this occasion but, as there was no answering sound from the interior, she opened the door and stepped inside, leaving her damp cagoule on the occasional chair in Kenneth's hall.

From the first she knew that something was amiss. On previous visits, when they had arranged the session, Kenneth would be waiting for her at the top of the stairs, naked and lustful. On those occasions when she hadn't been able to give an exact time of arrival, or if he had popped out for any reason, he would always leave a note for her on the hall stand. But today there was neither Kenneth nor note.

Only a breathless, unignorable silence. More alarming still was the acrid smell which permeated the house, quite different from the faint aroma of lavender that usually greeted visitors.

When she pulled open the kitchen door, she saw the reason.

Kenneth's inert form was slumped over the breakfast table, one hand seemingly grasping for an overturned glass lying next to an empty vodka bottle. Both bars of the electric fire were still glowing, etching the folds of Kenneth's pale bathrobe in scarlet and keeping the heat in the room at furnace strength. Opened packets of paracetamol were scattered around, their paper wrappings marooned in pools of Kenneth's drying vomit.

Juliet was not given to histrionics. Nor was she afraid of death. She turned off the hissing voice recorder and slipped it into her pocket. Then she picked up an envelope from the table and stored that inside her jacket. Finally she opened a window, turned off the fire, filled a bowl with soapy water, pulled her lover's torso upright and gently slipped his bathrobe from his shoulders.

Then set to work, preparing his body for the autopsy.

* * *

Harris put his head round Plover's door. "I've got the blow-ups from the Polegate Car Park CCTV, sir. You said you wanted to check them."

"Yes, gib me dem here," said Plover, sniffling noisily, his new-found nasal twang making him sound like a

Bowery bum. He reached across the desk for a packet of paper handkerchiefs and sneezed.

"Bless you," said Harris.

Plover took the photographs and studied them for a moment.

"Dis is de same registration number?"

"Yes, sir," pointing to the time fuzzily printed in the corner of the photograph. "It's the only vehicle that left the car park in that time slot. We don't have a clear picture, but Wittington was almost certainly pushed out of it."

Harris pointed to a white blur, like ectoplasm, emerging from the offside of the vehicle.

"Driver must have thought that there was nobody that side of the station. Didn't realise the passengers were in Bowskill's shop. Keeping warm."

"Poor old Bowskill. He's been unlucky with dis business."

"I don't know about that, sir. He's decided to take an Eastbourne shop. They say he got it on very good terms."

"Not de shop they used to mess up Baxter?"

"No sir. It's in a better position and – "

Seeing that Plover was tooling up for another detonation, Harris prudently backed towards the door, "Is that all, sir?"

"Yes, dat's all for now." Then, before Harris could withdraw totally from the danger area, "I shan't be in dis afternoon."

"Quite right, sir," said Harris, ignorant of what the Inspector would actually be doing. "Get your feet up. Hot toddy in front of a roaring fire. Nothing like it. Do you good, sir."

He closed the door just in time.

From within came another major explosion, which sounded more like a roar of pent-up frustration than the symptom of a Winter chill.

* * *

It was a quarter to five when Julia emerged from Kenneth's maisonette, once more attired in her cagoule, and strode briskly away in the direction of the people carrier. Murray leaned forward to start the VW, but felt a restraining hand on his wrist:

"Give her a few minutes. She may be coming back."

But it was not Julia's distinctive vehicle that, ten minutes later, pulled up outside Kenneth's house. It was a police car, from which emerged two sturdy young bobbies who were later to describe events in these terms:

'Acting on information received [at 16.52] we proceeded as instructed to 72 St. Stephen's Road and [forcibly] entered the premises at 17.05. In the kitchen we discovered the body of a Caucasian male person [eyes brown, hair brunette] whom we estimated to be in his middle thirties. The body was attired in shorts, slippers and purple dressing gown. Body was seated at a kitchen table which contained a cup, saucer and drinking glass, together with a document marked 'Krunchers', which the deceased appeared to have been reading. There were no signs of a struggle.'

Meanwhile, knowing that it would be impolitic for officers from the Met to be seen at an East Sussex police investigation, Murray and Moon had quietly removed themselves from St. Stephen's Road and driven off towards Lewes.

* * *

Arriving that afternoon at Victoria, Clifford obeyed the guard's instructions, as he always did, making a thorough inspection of the luggage rack and the narrow space between the seats before disembarking with his one piece of luggage - a stylish cabin bag that Gwen had bought for him so that on the rare occasions he travelled by air he could carry on board his extensive collection of grooming aids. He found it equally useful when, as now, he was called to an urgent, albeit fictitious, professional conference in town.

As was his wont, he passed blank-faced through the ticket barrier, then with head lowered ascended the escalator and strode through the fast food hall to the side entrance where the taxis lurked. He gave the driver the same address he always gave on these occasions - an anonymous hotel in Bloomsbury from which Soho was but a step. His chosen hideaway was staffed almost completely by non-English speaking persons, who reacted as if they and their forebears had suffered a grievous insult if they were asked to carry a suitcase or to say what time breakfast ended. They could safely be relied on to thwart any enquiries as to whether a Mr Mollison had recently stayed there and what had he got up to.

Not that Clifford was expecting any such investigation. Gwen had long ago stopped showing any interest in these professional gatherings and if he were to slip up and she were by chance to find a ticket for, say, the Virago Gentleman's Club (an old favourite) in his waistcoat pocket, he was confident he could talk his way out of it ("Old Dicky Grampion – he's next year's president – insisted that a few of us went in with him, for a bit of a laugh"). So, when his taxi, having taken an unusually roundabout route - "Road Works, Guv" - dropped him off at the front steps of his hideaway, Clifford looked forward to two days of undiluted pleasure, with the South Coast murders far from his mind.

He was not to know that a couple of hours before his arrival, Dick Rodham, on a similar mission to his own, had also arrived at Victoria. He had also taken a cab, albeit to a different hotel, and was also looking forward to a furtive weekend of libidinous fun.

To their mutual embarrassment, the two met later that afternoon in a dirty basement room off Brewer Street, in an establishment catering primarily for devotees of S&M displays. Each was to offer a hurriedly-assembled explanation for finding himself in such surroundings, insisting that as they had an hour to kill and just happened to be passing when the rain had really started to pelt down each had paid the twenty-three pounds fifty admission just to get a bit of shelter. Both had professed to be in London only because of the demands of business. Neither believed the other of course, but they had to spend the rest of the day together in an expensive and meaningless pub crawl, to validate their respective excuses.

* * *

DI Moon had meanwhile made two calls to Plover, to assure him that everything was in place, and to tell him that her folks would 'move into position' when he had 'baited the trap'. Murray, overhearing these cryptic remarks, wondered why it was necessary to talk in those terms. Moon explained that their quarry was somebody who might have ready access to police phones and radio wavelengths.

* * *

Inside the Jackson-Grants' home, a silence had fallen between the two friends. Plod was looking awkwardly down at his knees. Ben had moved a few feet apart from him and was staring dully out of the French windows at the twilit garden. Snuff, registering that the throb of conversation had stopped, looked up briefly to assure himself that the bipeds were still there and, satisfied that they were, snuggled back down on to the flokati rug.

For an hour and a half the two men had talked, at times awkwardly and at times sadly, knowing that however dreadful their conclusions proved to be, the time for prevarication had passed.

Ben had owned up to his impotency and, even more painfully, confessed to agreeing to his own cuckoldry. With difficulty he had managed to tell Plod about the arrangement he and Julia had made with Kenneth Molloy. Plod had added something of what he had learned of the actor's homophobic tendencies since Soozie's visit to his office.

Gradually, point by point, the two of them had pieced together a scenario in which Julia and Kenneth had disposed of Fletcher and Baxter. It all held together. Yet despite the logic of the argument Ben still found it almost impossible to believe that his wife, a senior member of the Police Management Unit, so passionate and beautiful, could have simultaneously dealt in drugs and put two men to death.

Yet that conclusion seemed inescapable. The duplicity and guile of her, her two-faced wickedness, the depths of evil in the woman he thought he knew drained every drop of sensation from him. "I can't believe it," he repeated to himself.

As gently as he could, Plover offered the final, clinching piece of evidence. It was Julia's car that had been used to receive the drugs packages. There was CCTV footage showing that Helen Wittington had been drugged and pushed out of the people carrier in Polegate Station Car Park.

At length Ben spoke again, "So, you don't have any doubts at all?"

"None." A pause. "Nor has DI Moon." There was a further hesitation before he added, "And nor do you, I think."

Ben reached up from his wheelchair and slowly drew the lounge curtains closed. The room was now lit by a single standard lamp and warmed by the glow from the electric fire.

Plod continued, "Some details are still unclear but ..."

"There's enough to charge her. I can see that. It's just that it makes me seem such a bloody fool! Can't satisfy my own wife and so stupid I can't see that she is a psychopath and a drug dealer! What sort of a man is that? What sort of a copper? I shall be a laughing stock."

"No, you won't. She fooled us all. And remember there were two of them in it ..."

"No, Plod. One murderous nymphomaniac and one simple-minded toyboy. Why in hell didn't I see it for what it was? God forgive me! I was pleased because she seemed happier ..." He buried his face in his hands.

"The rest of us were blind. She was our boss, remember? And you suspected her right from - "

"That meant nothing. A good copper suspects everybody. Even his own kith and kin." He looked up,

"Yes, I thought for a moment I knew the figure that got out of the police car up on Beachy Head. When you've – been - close to someone - you can pick them out in a crowd just by the way they stand, move their shoulders, take a step. I thought for a second that it might be Julia – but then I put the idea out of my mind. I couldn't see how it was possible for her to drop me off, drive up in a police car and then pick me up again on cue. She had me for a mug."

"What about the night you were attacked? In your own home. You saw through that."

"I knew that was a put-up job. I didn't drink the sleeping draught – when you've been around a bit you learn what that stuff smells like. Then I heard the key safe open, and when he came in and got to work tying me up I could see his shoes. The old magician's trick. Screw your eyes up tight when they're putting the blindfold on – and open them wide when it's fixed. Then you can tilt your head back and see under the blindfold. That man was well dressed. He'd got fashionable leather shoes on. Not trainers. He wasn't a common or garden thug."

"Didn't you think that man might have been Molloy? And that it was Julia who spiked your drink?"

"Of course I did. Who else could have given him the key safe number? But then I persuaded myself it might have been one of my old carers. Or – oh anybody! - the truth was I just couldn't bring myself to suspect Julia. She was so bloody convincing when she came to rescue me."

"Why didn't you say anything to us on the night?"

"You know damn' well. Because you obviously thought I'd set it all up myself, just to distract you. I must have been on your list of murder suspects."

"You weren't."

"Well, you were certainly on mine."

"I was on your list? But Julia wasn't?"

"I know, I know. I was an idiot."

"Look. we've both made mistakes. The reason nobody saw Fletcher in uniform on the night he was killed was because he drove out of the station in Julia's marked car, on his way to a prearranged rendezvous with her. He was her designated driver. Now I should have worked that out. But I didn't. And do you know who did? Sergeant Harris!"

"Harris? You mean - duh?" Ben made a noise like a baffled Homer Simpson.

"Yes, that Sergeant Harris. The endomorph. My number two."

"We've been made to look like idiots."

"Worst of all was not taking Fletcher at face value." Plover paused and waited for a sneeze, which didn't come. "I thought he'd been killed because he had some secret flaw. Because he was a secret gay. Or a conniving druggie. In fact, he was exactly what he seemed to be - a straightforward young man with old-fashioned values."

"Who Julia pretended had warned her about the drug ring she was a part of?"

"Who then warned Baxter he was being set up."

"And sealed both their death warrants."

In the pause that followed Plover's smartphone bleeped. He took it out and stared at the screen for a few seconds. "They're on their way," he said. He crossed the corridor, turned on Ben's desk light and closed the study door. He moved back in to the lounge, leaving the door open a crack, turning off the standard lamp, then the fire, plunging the two of them into darkness.

They strained to hear any tell-tale sounds.

"How near are they?"

"It'll be two bleeps when they're drawing up on the road outside." Plover took out his smartphone and stared down at its faintly glowing screen.

Involuntarily, Jackson-Grant drew back so they were facing each other, one either side of the lounge doorway.

For a couple of minutes the only faint sound was the breathing of the dog on the flokati.

As his eyes became accustomed to the near-darkness, Ben could just make out Plover's form, alert for any sound. There was a faint crack from the electric fire as some metal component contracted as it cooled.

Waiting.

Then - a release from the tense silence. Two sharp bleeps.

"They're here!"

* * *

Sitting in the darkened lounge in Lewes, the two men tensed, forsaking the slightest movement as they strove to hear the arrival of Julia's car.

When the people carrier finally crunched up the gravel drive, it was for Plod an undifferentiated ribbon of noise. For Ben, the sound separated itself into segments of a familiar daily ritual – Julia cruising up the drive, Julia executing a three-point turn in front of the double garage, Julia stopping at the back door, Julia making sure she had taken everything she needed from the glove compartment and then – ah, yes, there it was! - the comforting slam of the carrier's door shutting.

There was a pause. Then the sound of the back door being, very gently, opened and just as carefully, shut. From across the room Ben thought he heard Plod sniffle and dab at his nose.

Willing them to walk up the corridor towards them. And to see the light under the study door.

Plod messaged DI Moon to put the police cordon in place. When they looked into the empty study Plod would effect the arrest. That was the plan.

They waited.

No sound from the kitchen. Where were they?

Then, unmistakably, the sound of soft footsteps coming towards them down the darkened corridor.

And suddenly, raucously, accompanied by a harsh rhythmic thumping as if someone were violently whacking the walls with a heavy cudgel, came the snarling voice of Francis Frog:

"It's ki- ki- kid's own Krunchers!"

With hatred and loathing in every syllable.

Then, as abruptly as it had begun, the voice was silent.

The footsteps halted. Although he could not see him, the slightest of sounds told Ben that his partner was tensing himself, ready to spring forward.

But then the plan went wrong. Awakened by the tinny rasp of Francis Frog's voice and aware that his Mistress was in the house, Snuff did what dogs do, identified himself and established his location with a loud, glutinous, unmistakeable yelp.

At that the lounge door was flung open and the ceiling lights slammed on. There in the doorway stood Julia, gun in her gloved hand.

The two men froze but Snuff, operating on the principle of enlightened self-interest, heaved himself to his feet, vibrated briefly and plodded over to her, tongue lolling seductively. Then, after a pause, sensing that she was otherwise engaged and that there was no immediate chance of a meal, he flopped resignedly down on the carpet.

As if to compensate for the dog's poor manners, Plover started to rise to his feet.

"Please don't get up Inspector." Still carrying the gun, she walked between them and settled herself on a Queen Anne chair by the French windows. "Let's not be formal." She took off her gloves and laid them and the gun symbolically on her lap, as if she were posing for a newspaper portrait.

"Where's Molloy?" Plover put the obvious question.

"You mean our Kenneth? Has Ben told you our dirty little secret, then? I'm afraid he's dead, killed himself. Couldn't face the music, as they say." She tapped the pocket of her jacket. "That was a recording. Not one of Kenneth's greatest roles."

"How do you – "

"How do I know he's dead? Believe me, he is. But everything is in order. I have informed your colleagues of his passing, Inspector."

She took an envelope from the pocket of her jacket and addressed herself for the first time to her husband. "I think you'll find his full confession in there." She went over and handed it to him. "Ben, you will know how to deal with that."

For a brief moment, as Julia stood by him and spoke his name, when he smelt her scent and saw her body so tantalisingly close to his, Ben doubted himself. All that tedious fact-checking, data collating, eliminating the impossibilities and coming to an improbable conclusion seemed like a parlour game and nothing more. This was the reality – Julia's hair and breasts, her soft lips, all the warmth and mystery of her. When she smiled her taunting smile at him, he knew he was at that moment capable of denying everything that he and Plod had so recently and so painfully agreed.

But when she turned away from him the spell was broken. A tsunami of revulsion swept through him. She was a sorceress. Those were the fingers that had pulled the trigger to blast a hole through Fletcher's head. That was the hand that held the knife that had sliced though Baxter's throat. This was the woman that had injected Helen Wittington with a lethal dose of heroin. So he knew, beyond all doubt, that Molloy's confession which she had handed to him would be nothing but a fake.

Beyond doubt she was guilty. Even though now, as she prepared to button up her coat and go out through the French windows, she seemed to be oblivious to the fact that the game was up and that she faced public humiliation and long incarceration.

As in a dream Ben saw her open the window and step through the curtains, saw her silhouetted by the powerful torches of the surrounding police, heard a faint voice ordering her to drop her gun. Then, silence. He did not even hear the sound of the car in which she was driven away.

He sat immobile, contemplating the enormity of it all.

Then came the supreme bathos. The silence was shattered by a sudden, roaring, window-rattling sneeze.

Snuff shot upright, startled, ready to leg it if they were under fire. Then, as the last reverberations died away, came a lone plaintive voice;

"Ibe so thorry Ben".

TEN

Julia's arrest closed the book on Ben's previous life. For a few months he lived his life in limbo. Once more attended by carers, venturing outside only to give Snuff a run around the garden, he saw a few friends, re-read crime detection novels and tried not to listen to news broadcasts. He had no more official contact with Plover. Nor did he visit Julia in prison, having been advised against it by Clifford Mollison. It was also, he told himself, because he wanted to remember the Julia he had adored and not the satanic hellcat she had, according to the media, now become.

Spring came at last. He heard that Mollison had resumed the post of secretary to the East Sussex Ornithological Society. Ben let his own membership lapse. But when the day was fine, he sometimes took out his binoculars and scanned the fields behind the house. One morning in May he saw a magpie swooping low over a distant patch of scrub land and was almost sure he saw a second flying in its wake. But he could not be certain. Either way, he refused to see that as a portent of his future. He tried to put from his mind the nightmare of the Winter months and endeavoured, not always successfully, to live in the moment.

The date of the trial was set. Julia Jackson-Grant (49) was arraigned on a triple homicide charge – the killing of Keith Fletcher, Richard Baxter and Helen Wittington. Seeing that charge in cold print, Ben found a new resolution stirring within him. As husband of the accused, he would not of course give evidence, but nevertheless decided he need not hide away. He would attend the trial. He told himself that he would not go there in any vengeful spirit. It was rather that attending these last rites would bring closure and might even offer the possibility of some kind of rebirth.

He began to make arrangements to attend, booking the unfortunately-named disabled taxi to transport him daily to the courtroom, making special arrangements with his carers and drawing up an expensive contract with two local students to look after Snuff. (DI Jackson-Grant however remained suspicious of anyone under the age of twenty-five and for the first days of the trial hastened home each evening to examine the dog for signs of malnutrition or torture. Finding no evidence of either, he gradually relaxed.)

* * *

Used to viewing local courtrooms from the safety of the witness box, Ben found the view of the Quarterly Sessions from the public gallery impersonal and forbidding. From the first moments of the trial – the swearing in of the jury, the entry of Judge Bamforth in her crimson robes, the exhortations to dispassionate consideration – everything suggested that the rituals of this Court were about much more than temporal justice. They seemed to embody a timeless wisdom, a God-like detachment far superior to mere earthy judgments.

In the midst of all this dispassionate ritual was Julia. When she first appeared in the dock, he could not allow himself to look at her. When finally he dared to glance across he saw she was a little paler, dressed in the kind of simple garment she would previously never have allowed herself to wear, but still straight-backed, still somehow superior to her accusers. When the charges were read to her and she was asked how she pleaded she replied "Not guilty" in a voice as clear and sharp as ever.

Almost casually, Counsel for the Prosecution – a grey-haired, sharp-featured barrister with a disturbingly loud voice – rose to outline his case. He gave a brief synopsis of Julia Jackson-Grant's career – her privileged education, her stellar success as a City manager, her marriage, her fundraising work, her appointment to the role of Assistant Commissioner, Police and Law, SE region – before turning to the charges before the court.

In November of the previous year, Julia Jackson-Grant's official driver, PC Fletcher, had seemingly overheard her on her car phone discussing an arrangement by which she would be paid a staggering £100,000 a year to act as a key operative in the South East for an international Drugs Cartel. Details of this conversation would be corroborated by DI Moon of the Metropolitan Drugs Squad, whose remit had then included monitoring such conversations.

Fletcher also overheard alarming plans to 'close down' one Colonel Baxter – a local character who supplemented his pension and fed the drug habit he had begun during service in Afghanistan, by selling small quantities of cannabis to some of the performers visiting Eastbourne's theatres. What Mrs Jackson-Grant did not know was that Baxter, a graduate in English, had made Fletcher's acquaintance during Baxter's service as a Neighbourhood Policeman, had been helping him with his studies in the Open University and had taken a special interest in his career. In spite of the disparity in their ages and backgrounds, Fletcher and Baxter were friends.

Fletcher, a young man with little experience of the wickedness of the world, told his friend Baxter everything he had heard, thinking only to warn him. What could be more natural?

After the luncheon break, Counsel said he had then to turn to an aspect of the case which members of the jury might find disturbing, even repellent. Mrs Jackson-Grant was undoubtedly possessed of an unusually high sex drive. All had been well with her marriage until her husband suffered a near-fatal motor accident, following which he was unable to engage in normal marital relations. This distressed both of them and – though it may not have been something he or the jury could ever imagine themselves agreeing to – they had decided she should pay another man to give her sexual satisfaction.

Unfortunately, she chose to buy the services of one Kenneth Molloy, a part-employed actor who advertised in the Eastbourne area as a paid gigolo. Sadly, whatever may have been his prowess as a lover, Molloy was unstable in temperament and distressingly homophobic in his attitudes. Mrs Jackson-Grant was to make use of these characteristics when she discovered that Molloy had fallen in love with her. So, as they made love, they made plans. First for the disposal of Fletcher, who Mrs Jackson-Grant thought was a dangerous impediment to her plans, but who she convinced Molloy was a predatory homosexualist.

On the night of his death, by arrangement, Fletcher drove the defendant up to a lay-by on Beachy Head. After a short while Molloy drew up alongside the police car in an old van, which the two had bought cheaply in Crawley and kept out of sight in Jackson-Grant's double garage. Fletcher was then by some means enticed in to the rear of this vehicle, where he was shot and his skull battered. Immediately afterwards his body was arranged against the stone wall at the back of the lay-by.

Fletcher's murder made it imperative that Colonel Baxter must also be dealt with, as Baxter would soon come to his own conclusions as to the identity of the killers. He was enticed into an empty shop in the centre of Eastbourne (we do not know how – perhaps it was with a promise of negotiation with the drugs bosses). What we do know is that Jackson-Grant and Molloy were waiting for him. His throat was cut, his limbs broken and his corpse crudely disembowelled. That same night – a Saturday – the two of them let themselves into the Devonshire Park theatre (the police had keys), disabled the alarm and roped the body, doused in deodorant and covered with an old white smock, into the mechanism from which the magic beanstalk would be unrolled at the following day's matinee. Witnesses would be called to attest to the truth of each part of this account.

As Prosecuting Counsel was speaking Ben stole an occasional glance at Julia. She remained impassive except for a wry smile and slight shake of the head. When Counsel moved on to the third murder however, her whole bearing changed. Her face was contorted with anger and at times she seemed almost ready to cry out.

"The motive for killing Helen Wittington," Counsel was saying, "proved very much less clear-cut. You will learn in the course of this trial that Miss Wittington and Mrs Jackson-Grant worked, as it were, for the same firm. We can only presume that Mrs Jackson-Grant was jealous of Helen Wittington's place in Kenneth Molloy's affections. The actress had after all been living with Molloy prior to his embarking on a career as a gigolo. The jury will also hear from another of his girlfriends testifying that Molloy had been extremely upset by Wittington's death. What is indisputable is that on the morning Wittington collapsed on the concourse by Polegate Station, having been injected with a fatal dose of heroin, she was pushed out of Julia Jackson-Grant's people carrier in a terrible condition. The jury will be shown the CCTV record of that horrifying event."

Counsel concluded by saying that the defendant was a clever and ambitious woman who would stop at nothing to further her own ends. But the jury would not be fooled.

At which point Judge Bamforth said that the Jury had been given much to consider, and that this was a good moment to adjourn.

* * *

It was noticeable that on the second day there were fewer sensation-seekers waiting for admission to the courtroom, and a faint sense of *déjà vu* hung in the air as if all that needed saying had already been said. Ben sensed the same feeling in himself. Prosecuting Counsel had clearly summarised the narrative Plover and he had agreed on in the previous February. There seemed little to add.

Defence Counsel, revealed as a snub-nosed, black-haired lady with a faint Belfast accent, began proceedings with a Statement of Intent. Too much of the Prosecution's argument, it appeared, was dependent on supposition and circumstantial evidence:

"We are being asked to believe," she went on, "that Julia Jackson-Grant was so consumed by sexual desire that she not only persuaded her poor husband that she should pay another for her gratification but allowed herself to be drawn into an obviously illegal drugs operation simply to bolster her finances. Moreover, when her role in that organisation came to the attention of her driver, and when he had passed on the information to Colonel Baxter, his friend and mentor, we are told that she plotted with her lover to commit two foul and premeditated murders. She, who was Assistant Police Commissioner for the area, and who had until then led a blameless life of public service. Is it likely, is it even remotely credible, that Julia Jackson-Grant would have behaved with such perfidy - and with such recklessness?"

She continued in this vein for some little time, stressing that Julia's commitment to charitable work had brought her much acclaim – witnesses to her hard work and generosity in local causes would speak to the court – and had led to her being made OBE. She had many times been in a position to make money from such causes, legally or illegally, but she had never for one moment given way to temptation. Quite the opposite. In the South East Julia Jackson-Grant's name stood for reliability and honesty,

"Ladies and gentlemen of the Jury, I now intend to demonstrate to you how easy it is to reinterpret the known facts. In the course of this exposition you will see how fragile the Prosecution's case against my client truly is."

"I rather think, Ms. Dancing," put in the Judge, crisply, "that your remarks are best saved for the afternoon session. The court will adjourn for lunch."

As he toyed with his red carrot salad, Ben tried to guess what impact the presentations might so far have made upon the Jury. He knew that research showed we make up our minds about people within half a minute of meeting them. So, had the members of the Jury already made up their minds about the relative trustworthiness of the two opposing lawyers? And about Julia?

In the afternoon Ms Dancing paid no attention to the preliminaries but called for, and then held aloft in her right hand, a cellophane-wrapped white envelope:

"Ladies and gentlemen of the Jury, this is the final testament of Kenneth Driscoll Molloy. It consists of five sheets of A4 notepaper and was prepared in the days and hours before his death. It is in essence a full confession by Molloy of his triple murder of Keith Fletcher, Colonel Richard Baxter and Helen Wittington."

"Its appearance months ago seems to have been greeted with scant respect. Firstly, although he was given it by his wife, Ben Jackson-Grant was so sure that it was a fake he did not hand it to the investigating force until they were assembling exhibits for the prosecution case in this trial. My Learned Friend for the Prosecution has had a copy for some time, but he too believes it to be a forgery, conjured up by Mrs Jackson-Grant in an attempt to prove her innocence."

"But it is not a forgery. I shall call an expert calligraphic witness to help me show you that beyond doubt it was written by Molloy."

"Kenneth Molloy's testament will be a central part of the Defence case. It will be our submission that far from it being something faked by Julia Jackson-Grant, this document was written by Molloy with the intention of saving her from having to carry the blame for crimes which he originated and helped to commit. It forces us to rethink many of the conclusions which have been drawn from the few facts which are before the court. For example, Molloy suggests that it was him, and not Julia, that Ben Jackson-Grant saw getting out of the police car on that infamous November night. Molloy says that he alone put the body of Colonel Baxter in to the unwinding beanstalk mechanism at the Devonshire Park Theatre in Eastbourne. And he says it was he, acting alone, who fatally injected his former girlfriend, Helen Wittington, and he alone who callously pushed her inert body out of Julia Jackson-Grant's people carrier, which he alone was driving out of the Polegate Station car park."

"It is compelling, is it not? But we do not claim that Molloy's confession is the absolute truth. We only claim that it *could* be true. This case is so shadowy and uncertain that we could offer several other hypotheses which equally well fit the known facts. The difficulty we face is that, apart from the certainty of the deaths, in this case the indisputable facts are very few."

"And those indisputable facts are not enough to convict Julia Jackson-Grant."

* * *

Over the following days in the courtroom, Ben found his hold on normality gradually slipping. During the macabre events of the previous Winter, he had fought against the slightest suspicion that his wife could ever trade in dangerous drugs and kill men in cold blood. Then, when his one-time deputy, a man whose forensic ability he greatly admired, had come to just that conclusion, Ben had suppressed his deepest instincts and forced himself to acknowledge that in the light of the available evidence it was not just possible, but probable that his lover was a psychotic killer. According to Occam's razor.

Yet as the trial progressed, he was in danger of losing his hold on that probability. As witness followed witness and the same ground was repeatedly gone over in the same way, certainty leaked into speculation and speculation loosed dark coils of doubt. Even DI Plover seemed less than certain in the witness box and Clifford Mollison took his professional caution to extremes, saying he could not be certain who it was that had first suggested to him that Fletcher had given Julia Jackson-Grant her tip-off about the Drugs Cartel. Soozie Wade seemed terrified of the court and confessed that she was uncertain whether Kenneth Molloy was grieving for Helen, or whether his unhappiness had another, unknown cause.

DI Moon did not appear until the fourth day and, in view of the upcoming trial of the Drugs Cartel bosses, the Judge so limited her testimony that she seemed to contribute nothing to the prosecution. Indeed, she may have unwittingly detracted from it, as Defence Counsel quizzed her hard over the conversation between Julia and the Drugs bosses that she claimed to have overheard. "Looking over the transcript of that conversation," Ms. Dancing asked, "can you be quite certain the Assistant Commissioner is not leading the caller on, allowing him to incriminate himself?" DI Moon said that she could not, of course, be absolutely certain. At this Ben allowed himself a peep at Julia and could almost have convinced himself that her face bore a fleeting look of triumph.

The witness who made the most powerful impression on the court was Errol Gooch, a short bald actor widely known as 'Albert Muckle' - the name of the warm 'earted street-trader he played in an inexplicably popular TV soap about life in the Birmingham back streets. He told the court that on a shoot for that show Molloy had, without provocation, criminally assaulted him off-set, when he was resting between scenes. Under cross-examination he indignantly denied that he had lured Molloy to his dressing room hoping to make a sexual conquest. Judge Bamforth who seemed, unexpectedly, to be well-acquainted with the actor's work, congratulated Gooch on coming forward and voluntarily doing his public duty without thought for his reputation. Of course, it was the Judge's approving comments that were most frequently quoted in the following day's newspapers - beneath Gooch's smiling *Spotlight* portrait.

The two expert witnesses had less media impact than 'Albert'. The first was a graphics expert, Dr Sun May Lee, who testified that Kenneth Molloy had personally written his confession but declined to speculate on his state of mind when he wrote it. Nor was she willing to summarise Molloy's character from his handwriting. Indeed, she was scornful of so-called experts who claimed to be able to do this, terming it a 'fortune cookie' science.

She would certainly have termed the second expert a 'fortune cookie' scientist. He was a willowy Professor of Sexology from an obscure university in the Midlands, with glossy black hair and the pasty features of a silent-film star. There was something of the twilight world about him, an impression reinforced by the fact that when he entered the witness box he carefully placed a black bowler hat on the ledge before him. He had comic potential too, for when he took the oath it was apparent that he spoke in a squeaky Cockney accent, like a drunken ventriloquist's doll. The effect was unfortunate because it rather diverted the court's attention from what he was saying about the relationship between sexual obsession, lack of emotional empathy and addictive violence. Unfortunate, as he was trying to emphasise that there was no causal relationship between the three states. The court only paid him full attention when Defence Counsel asked whether it was possible for someone deeply involved in charity work and with a high commitment to public service also to be a psychotic killer? It only took a moment for the professor to reply, with some emphasis, "I think it is *extremely* unlikely."

Defence Counsel started to ask him about homophobia but Judge Bamforth intervened to tell her that Kenneth Molloy was not on trial in her court and his written testimony could be quoted only insofar as it directly involved her client. Again, Ben stole a surreptitious glance at Julia and this time she was smiling her quizzical, thin-lipped smile, as if judge, jury and barristers were cardboard cut-outs in a toy theatre, and as if the trial was being enacted solely for her amusement.

The final submissions, repeating and emphasising all that had gone before, passed by as in a dream. Soon the Judge was summing up. As he heard the familiar parade of 'ifs' and 'buts' Ben was once more gripped by the fear that the patterns that he and Plod had thought they discerned were illusory, spider's webs delicately spun but too easily torn apart. There were so many doubts that he wondered why the two of them had ever persuaded themselves into being so certain. Here in the courtroom all attempts to categorise behaviour with any certainty seemed tentative and illusory.

He feared, as he sat listening to the precise tones of the Judge, that after all there were no certainties in this world, that the distinction between guilt and innocence was no more than a verbal fancy and that the transition from ignorance to knowledge merely a linguistic trick. Our attempts to sort out and understand experience are doomed to failure. And the biggest pretence of all is that a sense of moral justice is the distinguishing characteristic of *homo sapiens*.

Judge Bamforth was now telling the jury to retire and consider their verdict. When they had filed out Julia left the witness box, still sandwiched between her warders. He tried, unavailingly, to make himself believe this was a critical moment, that his life was now going to change, for ever. But he couldn't do it. It still felt unreal, the first rehearsal of a play without an ending.

Though he had been in enough courtrooms to know that when the Jury returned quickly it meant they had followed the Judge's directions and were going to deliver an uncontroversial verdict. The longer they were out, the more uncertain the outcome. Accordingly, as the gowned members of the court shuffled their files, whispered and fidgeted, Ben was surprised, when he finally allowed himself to look down at his overactive watch dial, to discover that already an hour had passed.

Could it possibly be that the jurors had seen through Ms Dancing's wiles and realised that the Prosecution had argued the case beyond reasonable doubt? Or had they seen through the mellifluous Prosecuting Counsel? He told himself that if Julia were found guilty he would expiate his guilt publicly. He would stand by her, put aside all thoughts of divorce, visit her regularly in prison and even seek some sort of spiritual redemption.

He realised, in a moment of self-revelation, that he was utterly in thrall to her, terrified by what had been revealed as her ruthless and vindictive nature, but no more capable of resisting her than a moth can resist a candle flame.

On the afternoon of the following day, it was announced that the Jury was returning.

As the jurors filed back Ben looked into each face for clues about their verdict, but there was nothing there save for the guilty self-importance of little people who have unexpectedly found themselves in the position of passing judgement on their fellow beings. Julia was brought back into court. The Judge settled herself back in her perch, glancing over to make sure the defendant had not substantially altered her appearance while she had been out of sight.

The Foreman of the Jury, a pasty-faced man in a bulging grey suit, identified himself and was asked, in respect of the first of these charges, the murder of PC Keith Fletcher, how had they found the defendant?

The one addressed exactly fitted the stereotypical image of the man-in-the-street experiencing his fifteen minutes of fame. He did not answer the Clerk's question immediately but held the agonising pause that precedes the announcement of *Best Film* at Cannes, or the winner of *Strictly Come Dancing*. Holding a scrap of paper in front of him, he bobbed his Adam's apple a couple of times and then said in a rush of sound, "Nogguilty". He gave the same answer in the same fashion when asked about the other two charges. The Judge then told Julia that she was free to go and, with the same note of weary fatality, absolved the Jurors from service for five years.

So ended the masque. Ben stayed unmoving in his electric wheelchair, drained of emotion. After a couple of seconds, he allowed himself to look over at the witness box. Julia, free of her guards, was still standing at its front, looking directly across at him, her eyes glistening. The hands holding the front rail were shaking slightly.

He yearned for a sign. Something to draw him out of this spiritual void. Could their trust and affection ever be rekindled? Or were they doomed to descend into a hell of mutual attrition?

He looked across, willing a response.

And Julia smiled her thin, equivocal smile.